"Why did I ... you of all ...

Brett was sure she knew the answer. "You want what I've now got, Jay," she said sadly.

"I surely do," Jay whispered, drawing her onto the bed.

"And what you want you think you have the right to take!" Brett was panicking, her own excitement barely under control. "How you Carradine men relish your male power. Well, you're not going to use me!"

Jay's eyes flashed as he released her. "And what do you want, Brett? You're a very rich young woman now."

"Are we dealing, Jay?"

"We are." He traced a finger along her cheekbone.

"Marriage. What do you say to marriage, Jay?"

"I can't deny that I want you, but I also want power," Jay said. "All right. I won't ravish you as I desperately want to, and you'll marry me, let me act for you in all things and bear my children."

Margaret Way takes great pleasure in her work and works hard at her pleasure. She enjoys tearing off to the beach with her family on weekends, loves haunting galleries and auctions and is completely given over to French champagne "for every possible joyous occasion." Her home, perched high on a hill overlooking Brisbane, Australia, is her haven. She started writing when her son was a baby, and now she finds there is no better way to spend her time.

Books by Margaret Way

Don't miss any of our special offers. Write to us at the following address for information on our newest releases.

Harlequin Reader Service
901 Fuhrmann Blvd., P.O. Box 1397, Buffalo, NY 14240
Canadian address: P.O. Box 603,
Fort Erie, Ont. L2A 5X3

Diamond Valley

Margaret Way

Harlequin Books

TORONTO • NEW YORK • LONDON
AMSTERDAM • PARIS • SYDNEY • HAMBURG
STOCKHOLM • ATHENS • TOKYO • MILAN

Original hardcover edition published in 1986
by Mills & Boon Limited

ISBN 0-373-02832-6

Harlequin Romance first edition April 1987

Copyright © 1986 by Margaret Way.
Philippine copyright 1986. Australian copyright 1986.
Cover illustration copyright © 1987 by Will Davies.
All rights reserved. Except for use in any review, the reproduction or utilization
of this work in whole or in part in any form by any electronic, mechanical
or other means, now known or hereafter invented, including xerography,
photocopying and recording, or in any information storage or retrieval system,
is forbidden without the permission of the publisher, Harlequin Enterprises
Limited, 225 Duncan Mill Road, Don Mills, Ontario, Canada M3B 3K9. All the
characters in this book have no existence outside the imagination of the
author and have no relation whatsoever to anyone bearing the same name
or names. They are not even distantly inspired by any individual known
or unknown to the author, and all incidents are pure invention.

The Harlequin trademarks, consisting of the words HARLEQUIN ROMANCE
and the portrayal of a Harlequin, are trademarks of Harlequin Enterprises
Limited; the portrayal of a Harlequin is registered in the United States Patent
and Trademark Office and in the Canada Trade Marks Office.

Printed in U.S.A.

CHAPTER ONE

BRETT stood on the upper balcony of the homestead and watched the Beech Baron soar over the edge of the escarpment and begin its descent into Diamond Valley.

Jay would be at the controls. Morton and Elaine would be hunched up in tense discussion behind him.

John Carradine had two sons, but only one of them could replace him. John Benjamin Carradine was a brilliant and extraordinary man; he had built up a great pastoral empire. Now he lay dying, and his sons were returning to divide up the spoils.

And I'm one of them, Brett thought with a shuddering, dry sob. She had gradually stopped crying, knowing the family were coming and she would have to be strong.

Whatever she did she was a Carradine possession. It had begun when she was a small child and in time John Carradine had assumed complete authority over her life. Carradine money had sent her to boarding school, then on to university. She had a degree now, but as yet, no job. She was barely twenty and still dependent upon the man many people believed to be her father.

'There's something about her that reminds me of J.B.!' one of the Carradine cousins had whispered to another, and the ten-year-old Brett had reported it to her mother as very strange. How could *she* remind anyone of Mr Carradine? Mr Carradine was the god in their lives.

That was the first time she had ever become aware of the terrible aura that surrounded her and her mother. And yet her mother was so beautiful: dark hair, luminous grey eyes, fine patrician features. Her young widowed mother had been appointed housekeeper to the great station after the boys' ailing mother had died.

It had bitterly offended the very best people, which of course included all the Carradine cousins. The only recommendation Brett's mother had had was the fact that her late husband had been a Carradine employee. Her physical beauty had given rise to a lifetime of speculation and gossip.

The stories were legion. Brett had heard them all and had been hurt by every one of them. Only J.B. was beyond common gossip. Beyond considering marrying Brett's mother. If she had been his mistress, and not even the most charitable soul had considered that she hadn't been, the underlying message was appallingly clear: even in the grip of obsession Carradine men only married women of their own social standing. Beauty appealed to them greatly, but there was never any danger that their hearts would dominate their heads.

Yet Brett had been treated extremely well— perhaps because, like her mother, she possessed that disturbing beauty. If John Carradine rarely showed love or affection to his two sons, he had showered it on Brett. Such perversity was cruel, and much as Brett had wished it otherwise, his tender indulgence had greatly diminished her chances of ever being liked or accepted by his sons.

Morton had veered between being overbearingly haughty or a cruel tease. Jay, that strange mixture, had protected her without ever showing the slightest interest. Jay was handsome, arrogant, high-mettled. He was forever at odds with his father, but his particular creed didn't allow him to direct anger or resentment at a mere girl; he was too much the quintessential male.

As a small girl Brett had idolised him with a woman's fervour; as an adolescent she had retreated behind a deep veil of reserve. Unlike her tragic mother Brett did not wear her heart on her sleeve. There was a hard knot of pain deep inside her that would never become untied. For all J.B.'s indulgence the humiliations of her childhood had made her fiercely protective of her own status and identity. Self-respect was all-important to her. If the conditions of her mother's life had made her subordinate to a rich and powerful man, Brett thought she would rather die than pay the same price. Yet hadn't her mother been trapped? Trapped by love and a small child. From the age of ten Brett had decided her life would be different, and such was the force within her small breast that she had made people, even her mother, start calling her 'Brett'. She had been christened Marisa Elizabeth Sargent. Her father, the man who *had* married her mother, had been called Brett. So Brett she was and Brett she stayed. No one had ever asked her about her extraordinary decision.

Now she stood on the balcony, slender arms clenched around her tense body. The Baron made a perfect touch-down and began to taxi along the all-weather strip to the great silver hangar that was out of Brett's sight. A chain of electrical storms had delayed their arrival and the western sky was still banked up with great curling clouds of purple-black laced with silver. She had flown through electrical storms two or three times with Jay and she had never forgotten the experience.

Nothing seemed to beat him, even the elements. Diamond Valley had once belonged to the Chase family and it was still said John Carradine had taken it off them unfairly. The boys' mother had been a Chase. The story was that she had surrendered an impossible life when Morton was about twelve and Jay two years younger, not long before the time Brett had been born. Morton favoured his mother's side of the family when the Chase family worshipped the alien, Jay. Jay was meticulously fashioned in his father's image, right down to the dark, stormy good looks and dazzlingly blue eyes. It was quite, quite extraordinary that they had never agreed. Sometimes Brett thought it was because J.B. feared his own son. Morton he could dominate; Jay he never could. Jay's rebellion, according to his father, had started when he was one day old. Jay too had idolised the mother he had lost, and his father's indifference to her had tempered all his perceptions. Between the two men a strange love-hate existed.

Yet Jay was the only one to love the station with a passion, though these days Diamond Valley was only a small part of the Carradine Corporation. The two brothers headed the top companies that made up the corporation, but John Carradine possessed majority stock in each company, ceding only nominal power to his sons. An empire that had begun with horses and cattle now encompassed aviation, real estate and mining.

Jay had walked out on his father a dozen times, but each time that proud and ruthless despot had effected a reconciliation. No one ever knew for sure if emotion played a part in it or if J.B. knew his son was far too valuable to the Corporation to lose. There were rival companies desperate for men of Jay's outstanding calibre. Jay always further outraged his father by pointing out that he was only looking after his mother's money. There was too much truth in it for even J.B. to explode. It was an open secret that John Carradine had seized on what was left of his wife's personal fortune, even if his brilliant strategies had made it grow beyond anyone's imaginings.

Lightning struck in a vivid flash and Brett turned away with a wince of pain and grief. Of all of them she had been the only one John Carradine had turned to. She had been offered a minor academic position with the History Department but been forced to reject it so that she could return to Diamond Valley. For better or worse she was caught by her love for the man who had been her own and her mother's protector. Instinct told her he was not her father, and both he and her mother had sworn to her, her mother in anguish, J.B. with great sadness, that all the gossip was totally unfounded.

'There's nothing in this world I'd love more than to be able to claim you for my daughter,' he had told her. 'You are the daughter of the only woman I have ever loved and in that way you are my daughter too. This I swear.'

For the past two months, Brett had watched the

man she called J.B. die by inches. With almost his last strength he had attempted to engineer a fatal accident, but though he had worked it out boldly, chance worked against him. After that he lacked the strength to drive or ride and was confined to his bed with a nurse in full-time attendance.

It was a terrible way for anyone to die, and all the more pitiable in such a vigorous man. From a big, rangy man well over six feet he had wasted away with a cancer, accepting much less medication than he needed so he could be alert to talk to Brett. Often at two or three in the morning when the trauma seemed the worst, as Nurse Reed put it, Brett was always on call, but whatever was required of her seemed little enough. John Carradine was a legendary figure in her life, the only father figure she had really known, and his need for her presence was ferocious.

Her presence or her mother's? He often called her Marian. With such a depth of feeling in his heart Brett could never accept why he had chosen to throw such a dark shadow over all their lives. Her mother had not only been beautiful, but gentle and refined. She had never been good enough to become the second Mrs Carradine. Such rejection, for whatever reason, had affected Brett profoundly. No matter how much a woman could come to love a man, she could never trust him.

It would take about ten minutes for them to get up to the house. Brett turned away from her blind contemplation of a magnificent sky and walked into her bedroom. It was as beautiful and softly formal as if it belonged to a true daughter of a historic homestead. Her canopied bed was a Georgian four-poster, the fall-front secretaire was French and the lovely still life over the white marble fireplace was eighteenth-century Dutch. She was recognised but never accepted.

Brett turned and looked at her reflection. In contrast to her magnolia pale skin her hair looked very dark, almost black. Her eyes were grey; large with a strange luminous quality. She never knew if she was beautiful or not. She wasn't pretty. There was a certain aloofness about her features, yet her looks made an impact. As much a part of her as a destructive mystique had been part of her mother. She wasn't tall, in fact she was petite and slender enough to float away. Her outward demeanour was one of cool, swan-like composure. Inside did not necessarily coincide. All her life she had been kindly treated by a rich and powerful man. Inside her burned a wish for freedom.

Alice Reed, the nurse, was just coming out of the master suite when Brett moved down the long gallery.

'He's asleep,'she whispered, giving Brett a smile full of warmth and comfort. 'I heard a plane. Is that the family?'

'Yes.' Brett hoped that her nervous tension wasn't showing. 'They should be here in a minute. Toby was standing by to drive them up. Mr Morton Carradine is bringing his wife.'

'I see. Nurse Reed, a pleasant, competent-looking woman in her mid-forties, only nodded. She had met Elaine Carradine only once and given the option would choose not to have to meet her again.

'We'll take it as serenely as we can,' murmured Brett. 'Mrs Carradine may not have been happy that I chose you, but I'm sure she's been made aware that you've been wonderful with Mr Carradine and great support to me.'

'Don't worry, dear,' Alice Reed put out her hand and patted the girl's delicate right shoulder. 'I'll just keep out of the way. Dinner with Mrs Mac in the kitchen. I'm used to difficult people. My only concern is my patient. *And* you. You've borne the brunt of it, you know. All those broken nights are beginning to tell. There are shadows under those big eyes.'

Brett reached the landing of the great divided staircase just as the family moved into the entrance hall. Morton, a handsome, slightly fleshy blond giant, was frowning, and though the equally blonde Elaine looked up, she didn't bother to acknowledge Brett's presence. Toby was staggering under the weight of four very expensive pieces of luggage, and there was no sign of Jay.

'What is it this time, Brett?' Morton demanded. 'Another false alarm?'

'Your father is dying, Morton,' Brett answered quietly.

'Tell us again at the next summons,' added Elaine in her sharp, brittle fashion. 'Travelling makes me so irritable.' She looked down in disgust at the impeccable freshness of her yellow linen pant-suit. Elaine had been a society girl turned top fashion model before her marriage. If anything her image was even more brilliant.

'Where's Jay?' Brett's luminous grey eyes went beyond them.

'What's it to you, darling?' snapped Morton. 'There's always been an odd little bond between you and my brother.'

'God, Morton!' Elaine gave her husband a furious stare. 'The things that occur to you, occur to nobody else! Jay doesn't take the slightest notice of Brett.'

'No?' laughed Morton. 'He's taking a look around, lake eyes,' he said coolly. 'You look like you might shatter at a touch. Nerves, perhaps?'

Brett ignored him and walked swiftly towards the door, and as she did so Morton caught her around her small waist, trapping her in a bear's hold. 'Don't play the princess with me, sweetheart. Hard to know how you developed *that* little touch!'

Behind the hostility was a barely concealed lust. 'Let me go, Morton,' she said tautly, her body communicating her dislike of him.

'About time you had a man to handle you,' he said jeeringly. 'Or do you secretly fear them?'

Elaine, eyes blazing, decided to take a hand, but before she had time to snap anything off, Jay walked from the fading twilight into the brilliant light.

'Brett?' His startlingly blue gaze whipped from his brother to her, his expression so taut Morton instantly dropped his arm.

'Take it easy, brother,' Morton cautioned in half-mocking, half-wary tones.

'I'm afraid young Brett here rather fancies herself as a seductress,' Elaine offered abruptly.

'Or good old Mort couldn't bring himself to allow her to go past,' returned Jay in a quiet, deadly voice. 'We're here because J.B. is dying. It's Brett who's sat with him day after day all these long months. I don't want anyone upsetting her in any way. Is that understood?'

'We don't want Jay to be cross with us, do we, darling?' Morton moved towards his wife and took hold of her arm. 'We'll go upstairs and get out of the way.'

'How is he, Brett?' asked Jay when they were standing alone in the silent hall.

'Going fast.'

'My God, is it possible?'

'It's very hard to accept.'Brett, overtired and overwrought, felt unable to go on. There was stark pain in Jay's eyes, a rare show of emotion on his dominant dark face. It affected her deeply, and Jay had to take hold of her shoulders so he could get a better look at her face.

'You're closer to him than anyone else.'

She shook her head, aware of the turbulence in him. 'He *loves* you, Jay,' she exclaimed with pained emphasis. 'He can't tell you, that's all. It's trapped inside him, unable to come out.'

'I don't require a special explanation,' he said cuttingly. 'Anyway, it doesn't matter now. Can we go to him? That's if he wants to see us at all.'

'Please don't be bitter, Jay,' she begged.

'Don't plead with *me*, Marisa.'

'Sometimes I think you hate *me*!' Brett sighed.

'Why would I feel anything so extreme?' His hands tightened with bruising strength on the fine bones of her shoulders. 'You're as much a victim as the rest of us.'

'I know my head aches.'

'Aren't you sleeping?' His brilliant, narrowed gaze moved over her still, pale face and dark cloud of hair. Her eyes were like great shadowed pools of light.

'He likes to talk at night,' she explained with difficulty. 'The pain must be at its worst then.'

'And what does he call you—*Marian*?'

'Don't torture yourself, Jay. Torture me.',

'*Does* he?'

'Yes.' She bowed her dark head.

'He must have loved her.'

'God knows. What's clear is he wouldn't admit that either.'

'Carradines don't take their housekeeper to wife!'

Brett turned her head up at his cruelty, but there was only cynicism and pity in his eyes. 'You can't escape your own bitterness,' he told her.

'Some must be inevitable,' she admitted. 'It can't destroy my feelings for him, Jay. Your father has been the power figure in my life. He's been very good to me.'

'Considering all the talk I should think he would have to be.'

'He's *not* my father, Jay.'

'I *know* he's not!' His dark vibrant voice had the crack of a whiplash. 'Whatever else you are, you're not my little half-sister.'

'Why are you so sure?' she whispered.

'Because I've examined and tested every feeling I've ever had for you. I've had plenty of time.'

'And there's no deep affection?'

'No. Nothing so simple,' he said bitingly. 'There's no blood tie. Just an unresolved ambivalence.'

His downbent gaze never wavered. It was almost

as though he wanted to break her, and Brett, tired and grief-stricken, lost control. It was shocking the power he had to hurt her. Shocking that he knew.

A little sob escaped her that she quickly smothered, ivory hand to her mouth. 'I see through you, Jay!'

'Yes, you do!'

Tiny little charges of electricity seemed to be exploding in her brain. 'You're cruel! You're planning some cruelty right now.'

'Not planning, little one,' he corrected. 'I'm going to pull it off.'

'And I'm certain it has something to do with me!'

'Isn't your real name Marisa?' He grasped hold of her delicate shoulders. 'Why don't you use it? Can't you *bear* to use it?'

She took a shuddering, deep breath. 'No.'

'Because you're certain about nothing. Can't you use your instincts?'

'And what are they supposed to tell me?' Brett raised her hands to her ears. 'That I can never look at you? That I have to look someplace else?'

There, she had said it, as he wanted her to say it. He had shocked it out of her. 'Why don't you leave me alone, Jay?' she cried defensively.

'And allow your conflicts to become a permanent part of you?' he held her still. 'You used the name Brett as a means of coping with all the anxieties ugly gossip aroused. In a sense you felt abandoned by everyone. Your mother, your real father who was tragically killed, your mother's lover, who just happened to be *my* father. You were an angry-anxious child, and you still are underneath the many veils of reserve you've developed. You still don't know who you are and you're still suffering from your fantasies. My father claims to love you, and God knows you'll rate a considerable mention in his will, but he could have set your tormented little soul at rest with a simple blood test. But no. As he came increasingly to care for you the more he allowed this thing to go on. He wouldn't legalise his relationship with your mother, and for all his strong feeling for you he's allowed you to continue frightened and insecure.'

'He *told* me he wasn't my father,' Brett sobbed.

'He could have done much more than that,' Jay pointed out harshly. 'How could anyone sort out their feelings about the man? How could anyone accept the many terrible things he has done? You don't really think he would have allowed you to take up your university post, do you? After all the care and attention that was lavished on you? More, in fact, than I'm sure he would have given his own daughter. Especially if she'd been a blue-eyed blonde. He didn't hold them in very high esteem. He didn't hold any woman in very high esteem, Marisa—your mother, my mother, you. All of you loved him and he played too large a part in your lives. Parental love he never gave. When *we* were kids, Brett, we were aching for love. Mort used to cry himself to sleep—I remember that vividly. I had my own stresses, but I was shaped another way. When you were a little girl, you wanted to love me in whatever role figured in your dreams. My father saw that, so he had to provide us with an insurmountable barrier; an anxiety so strong it was intended to warp our whole relationship. My father couldn't love me, and he couldn't bear *you* to love me. He did everything in his power to increase guilt feelings in both of us. There are rules about loving your half-brother. He knew *I* would never accept his cruel machinations. My father is like some ancient king, Marisa—he can't bear for his own son to have everything after he's gone. I know for a fact he was planning to marry you off to Lee Kennedy. He regarded Kennedy as a vassal he could govern. Both of you would remain dependent on him.'

Brett was beginning to feel dizzy. 'I don't believe you,' she whispered. She was afraid she was going to faint.

'Hasn't Kennedy flown in here at least a dozen times since you've been back?'

'To see your father.'

'Of course. And to see you. You've been so taken up with trying to find out who you are that you can't even see yourself. Your features have the purity of a little saint's, but your aura is all sexual. Men want you, Marisa. It's something very basic, even primitive which is why you're going to keep out of Mort's way.'

'How *dare* you!' Brett's smoky eyes were now smouldering with a small flame.

'You know, given just the slightest encouragement he would snap,' drawled Jay.

'Then you tell him to keep away from me!' Brett's angry cry spiralled around the empty hall. 'He's brought his wife with him, in case you've forgotten.'

'And he certainly chose poorly,' Jay gritted in a voice impossible to overhear. 'It's only women like you a man has to fear.'

'Like my *mother*?' The grief swelled up. 'You've never forgiven her, have you? She had so many names. You'll never forgive me—never, never.'

Brett put her white hands to her temples, and the sight of her seemed to incite Jay to madness. He scooped her up almost violently so that she inhaled the male scent of him. 'The evil is going to die with him!' Jay exploded furiously as her head fell back against his arm. '*I'm* here, Marisa, if you can't save yourself.'

Some time after midnight Brett sat up in bed in a panic. Someone was knocking on her door, and as she stumbled across the darkened room she heard Nurse Reed's voice.

'Brett dear, you'd better come. *Brett!*'

Brett had never seen Alice Reed crying, but she was crying now, her capable face weary and ravaged. Brett only turned to snatch up her satin robe, pulling it on over her long flimsy nightgown. She had lived with this moment for months, but it now came as a terrible shock.

They were all assembled around the bedside with John Carradine's personal physician in attendance. It was one of the most terrible sights Brett had ever seen and one she knew would be burned into her brain. By far her worst experience had been the afternoon they brought her mother in after her horse had bolted and thrown her. She had begun to cry first, then scream, and someone had taken hold of her and hidden her away in his arms. But not before she had glimpsed her mother's crumpled body, her white still face, the angle of her neck. The someone had been Jay.

Now as she stood frozen on the threshold in perhaps the clearest indication of her lack of true identity Jay held out his hand again. His face was a graven mask and it told her the end was very near.

'Did you really have to call her, Nurse?' Elaine demanded bitterly, and for once Morton sent her a glance, heavy with anger and contempt that shut her up.

'Brett's the daughter he never had!' he hissed in a voice that wavered, then cut out.

Brett went forward, the breeze through the open french doors lifting the hem of her long robe and fanning it behind her. Love had so many faces, she thought. Everything Jay had said was true, but still she wanted to kiss J.B.'s cheek, stroke the silvered hair from his fine brow. Whatever he was, whatever he had done, he had served as the only father she had ever really known.

As she moved closer to the bed, something stirred within the dying man and he suddenly opened his eyes.

'*Marian!*'

The shock was so great, the expression on his face so intimate, so radiant, she almost slumped to the floor. Much as John Carradine had called her by her mother's name, it was a kind of forgetfulness having its origin in the pain of loss. Now he truly saw *her*.

'Marian, my love!'

Brett didn't think she could move, trapped by that terrible, avid glance, but Jay plucked her up and almost lifted her to the bed.

'I'm here,' she whispered, the tears pouring down her cheeks. 'I'm here, John.' She supposed she would never know why she had called him by a name she had never used before.

'Please, Marian, don't cry.' He stretched out a hand to her and she caught it and pressed it against her cheek. It felt like paper, not flesh.

'I love you.' The words simply flowed.

'I didn't think I'd see you this side of the grave!' J.B. made a sound that was almost a harsh chuckle. He stroked Brett's shining dark head, then frowning fiercely, stared up at his younger son.

'Still planning to take her for yourself?' There was a peculiar, jarring shift to a crafty lucidity.

'Too bad you'll miss it, Father,' Jay returned impassively, his blue eyes blazing like gems.

'Take your pick of anyone else,' his father warned him. 'Marisa is not for you, and you know why.'

'You've lost control, Father,' Jay admonished him in a quiet, deadly voice of imminent authority. 'Can't you just die in peace with us all?'

'I'm sorry, no!' Something midway between a snarl and a smile bared the old man's teeth. 'I'll admit I always had a problem with you, Jay. You always had a notion to usurp me—unlike your older brother. One way or the other I've done it all wrong.'

'It's not too late, now,' said Jay in an urgent voice. 'I'll beg if you want me to.'

JB shook his head. 'You will, but never for yourself. I've only met another man as hard as myself, and that's you.'

'And I've got a lot of years ahead of me,' Jay said in a soft, tingling voice. 'Tell her, Father. You love her, don't you?'

'I never loved anyone else.' The old man let out a rattling sigh. 'Not a one of my family ever did understand. Your mother, she settled to keep

Diamond Valley. *Her* father sold her to me. 'Course, they didn't call it by that name. Very important family, your people, the landed gentry. A glamorous name, but they took the money. Your mother turned you against me, Jay.'

'You just like to think that,' Jay shook his raven-sheened head. 'My mother is the only good memory of my childhood. I couldn't do anything for her then, but I've been doing it ever since.'

'I know about your attempts to gain control, Jay.'

'Then you'll know how I've succeeded.'

'Please!' Brett rose urgently from her knees, coming between father and son. 'Please, Jay.' She put out a hand to him, aware of the tension in his superbly lean body.

Suddenly Elaine began to cry; great, wailing sobs. No one thought for one moment it was grief. J.B. had never approved of her and she referred to him only as 'that bloody old tyrant'. The sobs were ones of pure frustration and rage. No matter what, J.B. would never turn to his elder son. Not to Morton. His heir.

Yet he did, trying to speak, but his outburst, his last contest with his younger son had made him too weak.

'Dad!' Instead of a towering big man Morton fell like a stricken adolescent to his knees. All his life he had waited for one word of love and acceptance from his father, but John Carradine was demonstrating that he intended to die as he had lived. These were his final moments and still he chose to reject his two sons. Brett, then and now, was the focus of his attention.

Her slender body was trembling violently. She

was profoundly grief-stricken, the more because all attempts at reconciliation had been destroyed by what had gone before.

In his own way, John Benjamin Carradine had sacrificed every one of them, yet with a heart full of compassion Brett bent over him and kissed his brow.

Death was so terrible, so painful, she had tried to block it from her awareness, but it was here now in the Valley.

A few minutes later, it slipped in through the closed door. Not even an empire-builder could keep a permanent hold on life.

CHAPTER TWO

THEY came from everywhere for the funeral: politicians, pastoralists, business tycoons, family. The rich and powerful and a sprinkling of humble Carradine employees who somehow had managed to cadge a ride to the Outback stronghold.

The homestead was full of people, hard-drinking, hard-talking, most genuinely saddened and shocked, others openly speculative about the contents of J.B.'s will. It was common knowledge that John Carradine had adopted a strange attitude towards his two sons; all the more strange because John Jnr was held to be a 'chip off the old block'. It was even whispered that Jay Carradine through his better blood would surpass his father's grand achievements, and maybe even Morton would shape up, freed of his father's harsh control.

Amid all this speculation the old stories were given another airing, so Brett found she had to be very brave to get through the day. Many of the women had judged her mother cruelly, none of them having succeeded in diverting J.B.'s attention, so they were prepared to believe the worst of Brett now. Whatever her parentage, and opinion was divided, it was generally agreed that she had done her darnedest to engage John Carradine's affections and so gain a place amongst the will's beneficiaries.

Strangely, the most powerful female member of the Chase clan, the boys' grandmother, Lillian

Chase, supported her. Life was full of ambiguity and paradox, and though from most people's point of thinking Brett's mother had pulled the Carradine marriage apart (which simply was not true) the elderly Mrs Chase had stretched her tolerance to look kindly and even favourably on Brett as an individual.

'Nothing has been easy for you, child. Absolutely nothing,' Mrs Chase told her in a free moment they were together. 'You've given back all you got one hundred-fold. No one else could have coped with my son-in-law half as well as you did. Show a brave face to the world.'

Diamond Valley buried its own dead, but the Carradine patriarch had made it clear that he wished to be cremated and his ashes released over the shifting rose-red sands of the desert he had loved so well. There were great stories about J.B., and this was another one of them.

Towards sunset, when the western sky put on one of its legendary displays, Jay took the Beech Baron up and his brother went with him. No one else was invited and no one else wanted to go. Morton at that moment was content to allow Jay to assume his natural authority. The duel for supremacy would take place later, but it was impossible for anyone to think Morton would win. John Benjamin Carradine had thrown a shadow over the entire Valley, but his younger son was and always had been a free spirit.

'I've never enjoyed anything more than watching Jay stand up to his father,' Lillian Chase was heard to reminisce. 'It was the classic story of a shameless autocrat being defied by his own image.' At thirty-two, still a bachelor, devastatingly handsome with a

nationally known name, John (Jay) Carradine was
the kind of matrimonial prize girls only dreamed
about. Highly visible at any time, his air of tightly
leashed grief as he walked about and talked to the
important people and the great families who had
arrived for the funeral threw many a woman into a
passionate turmoil. They had come to pay their
respects to the father, not fall madly in love with the
wilder of his sons. Jay's open clashes with his father
made people value him all the more. For one thing,
people feared in the late J.B. a ruthlessness which
was entirely unaffected. To have stood up to him,
boy and young man, must have taken guts of a high
order. It was equally well known that the first born,
Morton, had been very nearly destroyed by but
somehow managed to survive his father's brutal
dictatorship. By the same token he was currently
held to be under the thumb of his grasping wife and
her family, giving rise to the theory that Morton
Carradine couldn't function without a high level of
control.

Only Jay Carradine was reckoned to be a big
enough man to step into his father's shoes, and it
was high time Jay Carradine took himself a wife.
This more than anything was the reason all of the
landed families that had them brought along a
marriageable daughter, praying those brilliant blue
eyes would fall on their offspring with favour. Quite
a few of these smooth, gilded girls had older sisters,
married now, who had enjoyed varying success at
securing Jay's attention, but not a one of them
believed they didn't have more to offer.

It was a strange funeral; almost a grand social
occasion, with so many people from so many

spheres of interest present. Anecdotes about the old days and the way J.B. had accumulated his vast fortune abounded, some sharp, some humorous, some sad, some charming. A Chase uncle, a much liked and very distinguished man, was a natural at telling stories, and he more than anyone evoked a vivid picture of John Benjamin Carradine as a young man. As he was a Chase some of the stories were delivered with an exquisitely malicious pleasure. Nothing had ever been so bitter for the Chase family as losing the jewel of their holdings, Diamond Valley. It was the Chase family who had blazoned the pioneering trail westward. The Chase family who had built the magnificent homestead which John Carradine had bought lock, stock and barrel, because as Mrs Lillian Chase once put it in private, 'he never had the taste to do it himself'. What he did have the taste for was money and power and the young and beautiful widow of one of his outstation managers.

No one who had ever sighted Marian Sargent, however briefly, had over forgotten her haunting beauty, and once again they were confronted by that same disturbing quality in her daughter. It wasn't simply a matter of a cloud of dark hair, white skin and eyes like crystal; there was a kind of thrall behind the delicate grace. Many dark-haired women do not wear unrelieved black well, but against the sombre severity of her mourning dress Brett's magnolia skin had a stunning purity.

It was early evening before the will was read behind locked doors in the cedar-panelled trophy room with its lavish collection of silver cups and plate and gleaming blue ribbons. The portrait over

the high mantel was not of J.B. as it was in the
magnificent library. It was of Charles Thornton
Chase, the boys' great-great-grandfather and
founder of Diamond Valley. Jay often said that
particular room had the real feel of the house and
looking up at the portrait of his ancestor gave him
great pleasure. Not that Jay bore much physical
resemblance to the Chase side of the family, where
blond hair, sky-blue eyes was the order of the day,
but for all that he was clearly the family favourite.
His grandmother doted on him and his uncles held
him up as a model to their own sons.

Now around twenty people sat about the spacious
room while Edward Cavendish of Cavendish,
Manning, Ward read out the long and detailed will.
Bequests were made to various institutions, chari-
ties, certain younger members of the Chase family,
the boys' cousins who had accepted Carradine
domination, staff who had given long and loyal
service, but the bulk of his personal fortune, as well
as controlling interests in all his companies, instead
of being divided between his two sons was split
three ways.

'My God, he can't *do* this!' Elaine all but
exploded in the electric silence.

'Doesn't it say everything?' Morton exclaimed
bitterly. 'He made her ambitious. He made her
clever. He would say things like "you've got a good
business head on your shoulders". All these months
she's had a lot of time.'

'Except they never talked about his will.'

'Do you know? Were you there?' Morton flushed
at the severity of his brother's tone. 'I can't accept
this, Jay. I don't see how you can either. To hell with

all the fool stories! Brett's no Carradine.'

'Mr Morton, Iplease!' begged Edward Cavendish in a distressed voice. 'You may be interested to hear that Miss Sargent has been in your father's will from as far back as the seventies when her mother died.'

'Not to the same extent, I'll wager!' Morton burst out violently.

'Perhaps not.' The lawyer looked uncertain and hooked his glasses back up his nose.

'Would you be quiet, Morton,' ordered Lillian Chase, in a frosted voice, 'and let us hear what else is in this surprise packet of a will.'

Brett got up and started to walk to the door, but Jay called crisply, 'Brett!'

She turned, the new heiress to a great fortune, looking not triumphant but surpassingly sensitive and proud. 'Yes, Mr Carradine?'

'Sit down.'

'Please, child.' Mrs Chase, looking suddenly old and frail, took a sip of water.

'If *you* would like me to stay, Mrs Chase.' Brett returned to her leather armchair.

It would hit her soon.

There was silence in the big, mellow room while the solicitor's rather ponderous, plummy voice continued to read from the legal document, but Brett remembered none of it. From a pawn to power. Many women had tried to marry John Carradine to secure what she had been given. The will could not be contested. No one had been in sounder mind than J.B. He had meant to give her the balance of power and drive an even deeper wedge between his two sons.

She left the trophy room in uproar. One by one

private planes and charter flights had gone off, but
the family were still in the house and several guests
who intended leaving first thing in the morning. A
scene had to be avoided at all costs. Morton and
Elaine had turned on her like jackals, and only the
cold fury of Jay's temper had silenced them without
preventing their devouring her with their looks. She
dared not defend herself. Not then. Later perhaps
Jay's wrath would fall on her. She had heard Jay
and his father vent a terrible anger on each other.
How could she hope to survive that? She wasn't
made of the same stuff, and she didn't want to be.
She was Woman, compassionate, caring, suppor-
tive, enduring. From childhood she had been
witness to and victim of terrible male anger and
aggression. If Jay turned on her . . . if Jay turned on
her . . .

Brett fled.

Mrs Chase sent for her about an hour before the
appointed time for dinner, and Brett, looking pale
and composed, went along to the master suite. J.B.
had never used the main bedroom after his wife had
died, preferring another of the twenty bedrooms.
From the earliest days Diamond Valley homestead
had played host to countless guests, as many as forty
at a time, and hundreds on gala occasions, camping
out, so there never had been any difficulty finding
something to suit.

The master suite was palatial, almost overpower-
ing in its Victorian grandeur, and Brett could
understand why J.B. had chosen cosier rooms in the
opposite wing.

Mrs Chase was resting quietly on the dramatic-
looking bed, and she beckoned Brett in.

'You're coming down to dinner, aren't you, Brett?' Grand lady though she was, Mrs Chase was entirely without the pretentiousness and arrogance that marked Elaine and her friends, for example.

'I thought not,' Brett responded quietly. 'I'm not family, am I? I'm not known to your guests.'

'I will see to it that you are.' Mrs Chase gestured to an armchair with a fragile, bejewelled hand. 'Remember what I said to you earlier. You must show a brave face.'

'I was trying.' Brett resisted the cushion at her back.

'I know, and I was proud of you.'

'Thank you. That means a lot to me.'

'You're shocked, aren't you? Stunned by what's happened?' said the old lady.

'I never expected anything beyond a mention. A little money . . .'

'Ah, yes, but he loved you.'

'*Why* did he love me?' Brett looked into the old lady's eyes as though she was afraid of what she might hear.

'I suppose,' Lillian Chase reasoned quietly, 'because you greatly resemble your mother.'

'I would think *you* would find that unforgivable.'

'My dear, how could I hold *you* responsible for anything? You were, as Jay often says, the innocent victim. Anyway, my daughter and the boys' father were never happy together. Oh yes, Sarah loved him, or thought she did, and my husband believed it would work out, but there is no substitute for passionate, obsessive love. The marriage was basically a business contract worked out between two men. Sarah was so dazzled she thought it was all she wanted. *She* wasn't all he wanted. She was sweet, good, generous, loyal. You would have liked her and she would have been good to you. She didn't have the power to haunt or take over a man's mind. It was everyone's tragedy that your mother did.'

'It's been said, too often, that he was my father.' Brett dared not look at the old lady's face.

'Nonsense!' Mrs Chase almost hissed. 'He tried to make you believe it even as he told you so tenderly that it simply wasn't true. From what I know of your father, Brett, what I've made it my business to find out is there was no question of a relationship while he was alive. From all accounts your parents were a happy and devoted young couple who rarely saw anyone as exalted as J.B. Their paths didn't really cross until your father was killed. Believe it, Brett. It's true.'

'Yet he made me equal to his sons?'

'Forgive me, my dear, if I say a lot of it was spite—spite directed towards *my* family and a desire not to have Jay outshine his achievements. J.B. was a very complicated man, a tortured man in some respects. Morton, his first-born, was a tremendous disappointment to him. He so obviously looks like us. Jay was fashioned in his physical image, but Jay has a strong protective streak towards women, and he championed his mother. You were perfect to lavish his affections on—a helpless and dependent little girl. Later on you genuinely commanded his respect. Quite frankly, Brett, I think you deserve it. The only thing of great concern to me is, how are you going to use your power?'

Dinner was a sombre meal. No one was hungry. It was appearances only. The only thing that really went down well was the wine from a superlative cellar and later the port, when the gentlemen retired to the trophy room for some hard talking. Nothing changed on Diamond Valley. It was the ultimate sexist society, Brett thought. Man was king and women were chattels under the old feudal system.

Mrs Chase led the ladies into the Music Room, a room she had redecorated and which she particularly liked. It was much smaller and far less formidable than the main Drawing Room and contained a collection of musical instruments and exquisite Chinese Export wall panels. At J.B.'s insistence Brett had taken all manner of extras at boarding school, one of which was piano lessons, and, innately musical, she had taken to them extremely well. How often she had played for J.B. in this very room, but it was no time for music now.

Brett excused herself on the pretext of a headache, and although Mrs Chase had instructed her to come down to dinner she accepted Brett's excuse without demur. Elaine was in a particularly malignant mood and there was no guarantee she would continue to control it. Brett was not a Carradine. She wasn't married to a Carradine and there was no way she was even fit to sit on the board of any Carradine company, let alone become a major share holder. Her sensational figuring in the will was in the minds of everyone, including the hitherto benevolent Mrs Chase, but there was no telling what anyone would say after she was gone.

'Why did you do this to me, J.B.?' Brett asked as she picked up the small silver-framed photograph of him that she always set on her bedside table wherever she was. He had been a brilliant man, nobody denied that, marvellously effective in so many areas, but he had been a failure as a father: rigid, inflexible, ruthless. Jay and Morton had completely missed out on the joy of life in their historic home, and Brett was painfully sensitive to the fact that J.B. had used her to hurt his own sons. It was shocking, but it was true. Her inclusion in the will and to such a phenomenal extent was a deliberate piece of barbarity. Spite, Mrs Chase had called it. In any event, an outrage.

Not normally given to taking medication of any kind, Brett swallowed a couple of painkillers and prepared for bed. There was no question that she could remain at the house, although she was part owner of Diamond Valley. None of the household staff was antagonistic towards her, in fact she had long been treated as the legitimate daughter of the house, but even that could change. J.B. seemed to have hit on the exact formula for ruining her life. When she got back to the city she would take legal advice. There was a price to pay for overnight riches, and it was too high. She had never felt so alone in her life.

She had been in bed an hour or more when the chanting started; a curious high moaning melancholy sound that swept across the valley. It was the station aboriginals, of course, marking the departure of 'The Big Man' from their lives. It was incredibly eerie and it upset Brett so much she put the pillows to her ears. Tears poured down her face and everything inside her cried out for comfort. She had always been so alone, so terribly, terribly alone.

Helplessly she drifted over to the window, looking out towards the tree-screen gullies that were the aboriginals' secret world. Strange to say for such a authoritarian man J.B. had shown a surprisingly egalitarian approach to the tribal leaders—just another of his perversities.

The cool night air was wonderfully sweet-scented with all the punjilla in flower and the moon so brilliant Brett could see the lagoons towards the south-east glinting like sheets of silver. Even the distant sandhills were sharply outlined against the soft purple sky.

Old Wongin, who was a mystic, was the highest ranking at such gatherings. Once he had been a dreaded Kadaitcha Man, the tribal executioner who dealt in strong magic, and even now it really seemed as if he had been given exceptional powers. In his own way he had the same power as the white man to whom he had been so intensely loyal. To the ordinary aborigine Wongin's every word, every wish was law. He was obeyed without question and at once.

One by one the lights went out all over the homestead and a few french doors, even shutters, tightly closed. The chanting would go on until dawn, by which time John Carradine's spirit would have been taken up into the sky. But the sound was very strange and upsetting, rising and falling as it did, stopping suddenly, only to begin again, so even the nerves in one's body began to twitch.

Smoke from their fires twisted up in a cloud, but Brett, who usually loved aboriginal corroborees and ceremony, felt distraught enough to run crying through the house. Such chanting was designed to protect John Carradine from harm on his long journey, but Brett thought there was a limit to what she could take. She had seen through these last months. *She*. No one else had been prepared to watch J.B. dying.

Underneath the ritual chanting the small drums gave tongue. Brett found herself tossing and turning with the ever-changing tempo. It was impossible to sleep—*impossible*, yet she tried to keep a firm hold on her deep agitation. The wailing was heartrending, carrying its stark message across the valley. A legendary figure would walk the earth no more. Through their ancient ritual was he being helped to the Sky World.

Brett lay for a while longer in an ever-tightening misery, then she sprang out of bed, fingers of moonlight picking out her slender figure in a nightgown so fine it appeared as insubstantial as a cobweb. One thing was clear: she wouldn't get a moment's sleep without help. She had no idea how much Scotch or brandy she had to drink to relax her nerves, but she would pour herself a large measure and find out. Just about everyone else at dinner had drunk enough to drown their grief.

She was outside in the long corridor, still dimly lit by wall brackets as there were guests in the house. She didn't need any lighting beyond the moon to find her way through the house. She knew and loved every inch of it. Did no one realise what Diamond Valley meant to her? It was in her blood; the great homestead and the million acres of a landscape so powerful it had struck awe into the early explorers. The lonely grandeur. It had entered into Brett's soul.

It seemed to her as she moved silently towards the trophy room that J.B.'s spirit still hovered in the house, and she even threw a swift look over her shoulder, feeling a sharp thrill of superstitious fear. That chanting was enough to fan anyone's blood to white heat!

The room was in darkness, but so radiant was the moonlight she didn't look to turn on the light. The vast collection of silver cups took on an eerie luminescence, and she swallowed dryly and moved barefooted across the velvety Kashan rug to the low sideboard on the top of which stood a number of crystal decanters, glasses, and the finest spirits money could buy.

Brett was no connoisseur. Anything would do to gain some temporary peace. For a girl who had just been given everything, she was trembling like a leaf in a storm, fearful of trespassing on someone else's wood.

Man had always been a hunting animal.

The Carradines, every last one of them, were excellent huntsmen.

Brett reached out her hand towards a square decanter, and as she did so a tall shadow passed before the tall, mullioned windows. It almost stopped her heart.

She spun around in a mindless, atavistic dread, hands fluttering to her heart, an agonised little cry stifled in her tightened throat.

The tall figure was coming towards her, blocking out her vision of the full moon. His feet did not seem to touch the ground, yet she knew the set of his head, the wide shoulders and lean-hipped, dangerous body.

'Jay?' She tried to speak, but her vocal chords weren't working properly.

To a mind floating out of control he continued not to walk but to glide, and so great was Brett's trepidation she thought she would faint.

His hands were on her, on her shoulders, and oddly she felt that firm, moderate pressure might force her to her knees.

'I would have thought you'd be scared of coming down here, Brett?' he challenged her in a perfectly controlled, mocking voice. He was looking straight down at her, turning her slightly so the moon fell on her lovely, upturned face and filmy-clad body.

'What is there to scare me?' Even her voice jumped.

'Me.' He laughed deep in his throat. 'I've been drinking fairly heavily.'

'I think I've come down to do the same thing,' she quavered. 'I've had a terrible time trying to sleep— the chanting is so unnerving!'

'We wouldn't want J.B. to get lost, would we, on his way to the Great Sky Country?'

'*Don't*, Jay!' She was shocked by the dreadful irony of his tone.

'Starting in already to give orders?'

It was more like the flick of a whip than a rap on the knuckles. 'I've been waiting for *your* wrath to fall on me,' she said quietly, and dropped her head.

'It hasn't fallen on you at all. Yet. So what are you going to have, my little . . . friend?' Jay turned away.

'Anything.' His mockery blasted her. 'I've got wheels within wheels going around in my head.'

'I'll bet.'His caustic humour should have shri-
velled her up.

'If you'll just give it to me, Jay, I'll go back
upstairs.'

'The hell you will!' He put the glass into her hand.
'You float in here dressed in moonbeams, now you
have to stay. Seeing you're part of it all. Part of me,
my life.'

She seemed to sway before him. 'I don't want the
money, Jay. I don't want anything. I'll see a solicitor
as soon as I get back.'

'My dear girl!' He gave a jeering little laugh. 'You
want a solicitor? Use your own. There are quite a
few on the Carradine payroll.'

Brett could smell the whisky in her glass and it
seemed to brace her. 'I had no idea what J.B.
intended.'

'Really?'He took a quick step around, all power
and lithe grace. 'I thought you had a tremendous
insight into my father's devious, manipulating
mind?'

Her white flesh flushed and she turned away, but
Jay caught her as deftly as a big cat with its prey.

'Strange!' he mused quietly. 'I can see your skin
change even in the moonlight. It's like a pearl,
incandescent. Come over here and sit down. We'll
parody a friendly talk.'

She couldn't allow herself to be so weak, so
foolish. 'It's a funny time for it,' she protested.

'You never let me talk to you earlier today. Of all
the people present you were the only one to keep out
of my way.'

'I had nothing to say.'

'I kept track of you all the same. I never thought

there was such a thing as a woman looking alluring in a mourning dress, but that's the kind of woman you are.'

He took her wrist and drew her nervy, apprehensive body towards the cushion-piled banquette under the tall bay windows. 'We'll drink a toast,' he told her almost cheerfully. 'It's not every day a little changeling inherits a great house.'

The pain was so great Brett couldn't even see straight. She was no butterfly to be pinned to a specimen board. She tried to wrench her hand out of his grip, but he jerked her to him so violently the crystal tumbler she had almost forgotten flew from her other hand. It crashed to the beautiful antique rug, where it shattered into colourless diamonds, and as she looked down in consternation Jay clipped at her, 'Don't move!'

His own glass banged down on a table and abruptly he lifted her, swinging her high in his arms. 'What do you weigh? As much as a sparrow?'

Just to be so close to him was a tumultuous shock. Something between sexual surrender and anger swept her. For years she had done little else but drink in the way he looked and moved and spoke; now she was engulfed by this shocking physical proximity. She could feel the radiant warmth of his taut powerful body, catch the aroma of the finest malt whisky on his clean breath.

He didn't put her down as she thought, but continued to hold her. 'Now this is something that hasn't happened in a long time,' he murmured, with humour. 'The last time I recall having you in my arms was five or six years ago when I had to remove you from an ill-intentioned horse. I don't think I've ever moved so fast in my life!'

'I *do* remember being hauled off. *And* blasted. 'She was afraid to be in the dark with him. Afraid to let her head rest against his shoulder. 'Aren't you going to turn the lights on?'

'Why?' He started to move with her. 'The moonlight is quite extraordinary. It's truly like being trapped in a dream. Here, try my Scotch. I'll pour myelf another.'

Brett tucked herself back into the corner, a terrible excitement, like an agony, pouring into her veins. She understood what he meant by a dream. She had been dreaming the same dream for years, one she would never indulge in daylight.

'Sure you can't move back any further?' he mocked her.

'Give me a break, Jay!'

'You mean you aren't getting enough?'

She closed her eyes and tilted her head back against the mullioned window. Her eyes seemed to be full of shining tears. 'I guess all you Carradines have a cruel streak?'

'You've been safe from me, so far.

'Don't drink any more, Jay,' she said weakly. 'I know how you're hurting.'

'You know all about hurt at that,' he agreed sombrely. 'You can't run away from it.'

'No.'

A silence fell between them, then abruptly Jay turned to face her, curled up as she was amid the silk-fringed velvet cushions. 'I tried to hate him, and it wouldn't work.'

'Hating is not the way.'

'So show me another!'

Brett saw the sudden flash of his eyes, the hard sensuality of his expression, and an answering passion spurted into her blood.

'You've got no rights over me!' She dug one narrow, naked foot into the plush seat trying to push herself back even further.

'Who the hell are *you*?' His brilliant eyes narrowed over her and he reached for her as she had always known he would.

'Jay!' She gave one despairing little cry, a tight-throated, fearful sound, but he drew her up along his body, his hands clasping her head as his mouth came down over hers in a voluptuous wash of hunger.

She was drenched in it, drowning under an invincible excitement.

The first time, she thought. And it could only happen once.

He was still dressed in what he had worn at dinner, minus his jacket and black tie, and she could feel the dark mat of hair on his sleekly muscled chest gently graze her soft skin. His heart was pumping strongly against her breast, dredging up that memory of her childhood when he had lifted her clear of danger.

I cannot get free of him now.

Jay pulled her further along his body, then half turned her so that she was lying between him and the padded back of the banquette, her slender legs stretched out.

'You can't get away,' came his dark, vibrant voice.

'I *could* give you a fierce shove.'

'What, *you*, little Marisa?'

'I *can't*, Jay,' she sighed.

'No? You can't just walk away from your fate.'

'*What* fate? You're crazy!' Her will was being defeated by the urgencies of her body.

'Look at me,' said Jay deeply.

'You've had too much to drink. You've admitted it.'

'I'd need a lot more not to know what I'm doing.'

'What you're doing is taking your pain out on me.'

'And you're not giving me a little help?' He ran a finger from the tender hollow at the base of her throat to the cleft between her half exposed breasts.

Her skin seemed to burn, not with heat but with radiance. She thought it might even be lit.

'We should pick up the shattered glass,' she said weakly.

'I'd rather make love to you.'

'I must be way down the line.'

'Not you, Marisa. You're a real winner. One would only have to look at you to know you were destined for the big time.' His blue narrowed eyes glittered at her.

'I'll *give* it away!' she cried emotionally.

'You're damn right you will. It's mine anyway. *You're* mine.'

'You're just like J.B., when you think about it,' Brett said weakly.

'Aren't you sorry you comprehended too late?' He lifted her up and away from the cushioned bench.

'Jay, what are you *doing*?' Her voice was high with alarm.

'Trapping you, little bird.'

'Wait,' she begged. 'Oh, *please* wait!'

'I might have been able to do that once. Not now.'

Moonlight spilled through the great stained glass window that began at the landing and soared up into the next storey. Jay carried her safely up the stairs and along the darkened passageway that led to the turret room he had occupied since he had been a boy.

No light remained burning in the wide room, but he didn't seem to need one. Enclosed by windows on four sides, the room overflowed with silvery light, the barley twist posters rising sharply from the pale coverings on the huge bed.

'So it's come to this!' Brett gave a mutinous cry.

'Yes, and you get in there as fast as you can!' He threw her so that her slender body bounced gently on the firm springs and she sat up rapidly, glancing this way and that for some weapon to put her hand to.

'That's enough!' He closed on her, pushing her back against the pillows. 'You made your choice long ago.'

She continued to try for escape. 'I would *never* choose you—I promise you that!'

'Very fiery, but I don't believe you. Why don't you admit it, you little hypocrite?'

'How you Carradines relish your male power. Don't think you're going to use *me*!'

He came at her so suddenly she almost screamed.

'Leave it, Brett. Don't say any more. I like my illusions.'

'And what will you call yourself instead of a rapist?'

A bitter smile crossed his face. 'I'm not going to

rape you, little one. I'm only going to keep you here all night.'

'And how else am I going to entertain you?' she hissed furiously.

'God, whatever you like.'

'You're crazy, Jay,' she said a little helplessly, checked by the stark weariness of his tone. 'It would be fatal to keep me here.'

'I'm going to do it all the same.' He unbuttoned his shirt completely and pulled it out. 'I want comfort too, Brett. Can't you believe it? You *lavished* it on my father.'

'That's not the same.'

'What's our relationship, then?' He bore her backwards.

'Jay . . . oh, please, Jay.' She was a half-second away from revealing her soul.

'Out of a hundred women why did I have to choose you?' he grated.

'You want what I've now got. That's the awful joke.'

'I surely do.'

'And what you want you think you have the right to take?'

'Don't be horrible, Brett.' His glittering gaze consumed her. 'I've caught you countless times following me with your eyes. Eyes are the windows of the soul, are they not? What do you suppose they told me?'

'That I'm just waiting my chance to destroy you. I really *hate* you, damn you!' She half lifted her body from the bed to hiss at him, half exalted, half fainting with the emotions that blazed in her. If she let him kiss her, explore her body, she would never truly be her own self again. She would twist in ecstasy, agony, beat her hands against his chest.

'Stop that, Brett. You'll only hurt yourself.' He quickly checked her, catching her hands and holding them above her head.

All she could think of was a hollow triumph. 'Don't you remember the old stories?' she cried starkly. 'If they don't stop you, *nothing* will!'

'Tell me.' Jay's voice dropped to a menacing whisper.

'You and I.' Brett turned her head violently along the counterpane. 'We are children of the king!'

His eyes flashed like diamonds and he turned her face forcibly. 'Let's settle that right now, shall we? All the old stories were lies. I've done everything in my power to help you distinguish fact from black magic. You know what my father was—the master manipulator. He gave you the truth, but he did everything in his power to prevent you from accepting it. I'm going to make love to you, Marisa, and *you're* going to decide what I am to you.'

'And what if it destroys us?' she whispered.

'But it will *not*.' He looked directly into her wide, distraught eyes and she looked swiftly away.

'I hate you, Jay!' It was a cry of love and rage and pain.

'Marisa,' he whispered against her mouth.

The agony turned to flowering. Limbs like tendrils seeking and gaining a hold on his head, his shoulders, his long legs. His body was the most exquisite weight, so wondrously real, his man-scent mingling with her own.

Had she a heart of glass it would have exploded.

Her anger had only been a prelude to passion, a feeble defence that faded into transparency. Jay was draining her mouth of the sweetness he seemed to crave, and a powerful exultation snapped the invisible chains that held her and caused them to break away.

There were a lot of years in her involuntary, headlong response. A sexual urgency that roared through her body. Her small pointed tongue darted around his sculptured mouth, taking a step nearer to learning his fabulous male body. She had never been so profoundly aware of what it meant to be a woman, the most desired of all creatures.

When his masterful hand claimed her breast she went utterly still, heart pounding, every nerve stretched so taut it quivered like a plucked string on an instrument exquisitely fine-tuned. Her nipples were like tight buds, so abnormally sensitive an intense thrill, like a jolt of electricity, shot through to her womb as he twisted them first through the tantalising veil of fine lace and a moment later with moonlight illuminating their delicate, naked contours.

'You're so beautiful,' he marvelled. 'Satin-skinned.'

Brett couldn't stop him—didn't want to. It was a powerful yet real disorientation. She was going back on her dreams—the times he had come to her at night. Yet her innocence had never allowed her this ecstasy. A phantom hand and a phantom mouth had never aroused such frantic, concentrated excitement. Sensation was inexhaustible as his male drive increased.

'We're doomed, Jay!' Her voice palpitated like a

wild bird's.

'Well then, we're doomed.' He sounded utterly uncaring.

'You can't afford this.'

'You want it too.' Only for a second did he lift away from her body.

'But there's a price to be paid for everything.'

'Sure there is,' he drawled. 'I've been paying all my life.'

'So when does the learning start?' She twisted her head so that her mouth was against the lean column of his throat.

'I've learned, Marisa.' He knotted his hand through her silky cloud of hair. 'You're the one who was tricked. I hold you in my arms and you flutter and gasp. I can feel the high throb of your heart, see the blood move in your blue veins. I could have made love to you when you were fifteen years old. You were ready then—a miraculous female creature just emerged from the chrysalis. Yet here you are at twenty, still a virgin.'

'You don't *know*!' she protested.

'I know. If you don't call *that* self-denial you can walk out of here right now.'

'Can I?' She rolled swiftly, lifting herself up.

'It's not so simple. I locked the door.'

'Then I don't have a choice.' She looked back at his handsome, mocking face, the insolent arrogance of his male grace.

'A choice. Let's see.' His arm snaked out, encircling her narrow waist and drawing her back to lie beside him. 'What about control of your voting rights? Mort will be sure to want to sell Diamond Valley. There are other areas, more lucrative areas we could invest our millions in. We don't need a desert stronghold any more, and it has too many powerful reminders of J.B. You can promise me to thwart him and dear Elaine on that.'

'And I leave here unharmed?' Brett stared up at the plaster mouldings on the high ceiling.

'What's harm?' Jay turned his dark head to her. 'My hand on your breast? Your mouth against mine?'

'So *you* assume control. What do *I* get?'

'What do you want?' He swung about so he was resting on his elbow.

'Are we dealing, Jay?'

'We are.' He moved his hand along her cheek-bone, the whorls of her ear, the pure line of her jaw.

'I never thought to see the day,' she sighed.

'Really?' His voice sounded almost normal, clipped and controlled. 'I've been expecting it for ever.'

'Now you sound as bitter as I am. How often, I wonder, did my mother lie with your father and wish with all her heart that he would honour her as well as lust after her body. Many, many nights, I'll wager.'

'My God, this isn't your roundabout way of telling me you're thinking of marriage?' grated Jay.

She ignored the black humour. 'Yes, marriage,' she said in a harsh little voice. 'Why not?' It had never remotely occurred to her before. 'Marriage in memory of my terribly wronged mother.'

'My dearest Marisa, you could have taught her a few lessons.'

'What do you say to marriage, *John* Carradine?'

There was a strange, rapt look in her great luminous
eyes.

'God damn it if you mightn't be a chip off the old
block!' he exclaimed.

'This is no laughing matter.'

'Little one, you sound as hard as nails.'

'I was taught by masters,' she said drily.

He laughed again. 'It's not as though I'm terribly
interested in anyone else.'

'Are you very sure of that? Kerri Whitman thinks
she's stepped back into the picture.'

'Kerri is a very attractive girl, no more,' he
shrugged.

'Oh? Didn't she follow you to the island for a
week?'

'It was ten days at least.'

'Let me up.' She drew her nails along his strong,
imprisoning arm.

'Not until I bring our discussion to a close. Tell
me in detail what you want.'

'I don't want *anything*,' she said flatly. 'I told you
that.'

'You're a rich young woman now. *Very* rich.
You've had no experience whatever of business or
control. you're just an innocent little babe in the
woods. I know you're a clever girl, but your world
has been strictly limited. When you weren't at
boarding school or university you were here. You
know nothing of the real world. Even Elaine could
eat you up.'

'Not for long.'

'Long enough!' he silenced her drily. 'You're
beautiful, and there's no way I can deny that I want
you. I'm even fond of you in my fashion. I trust

you're fond of me?'

'Not at all. In general terms I would say I find you both intimidating and dangerous.'

'And when have I ever hurt you?' he asked bluntly. 'Why, you ungrateful little wretch, I'd say I saved your precious skin at least one hundred times.'

'You were kind the same way you'd be kind to a stray kitten,' shrugged Brett.

'This is all very telling, but I thought we were talking business?—God Almighty, if they don't stop those drums I think I'll go down to the creek myself!' He sounded violent, twisting up to look out over the moon-drenched river flats.

'They're hammering inside my head.' She pressed back against the pillows.

'I'll shut the windows.'

'No. They still go on, and *I* have to go.'

'We'll go riding at dawn. It's the best time and it will blow all the nightmares away.' 'I *can't* stay here, Jay,' she protested.

'It must be a hundred feet to the ground at least. Anyway, I'm going to sleep.'

'So what am I *doing* here?' She sat up, pleadingly, her hands going out to him.

'Providing emotional support.'

'You're the hardest, most self-contained man I know,' Brett sighed.

'To a certain extent, I am, but I'm tied to you, in a strange way. Also, I love power. Marry me and I swear I won't ravish you as I desperately want to. Marry me and let me act for you in all things.'

'For how long?'

'You're too damned smart for it to take a long

time. Say until you're twenty-one.'

'How do I know you won't take all the money from me?'

'We'll have Cavendish draw up a contract. He's the soul of discretion. I won't take your money, Brett. I'll at least double it. But I cannot have my hands tied. You'll marry me and you'll bear my son. Is that settled?'

'I want time.' She heard the deep panic in her own voice. 'I can't give myself to a man I don't love.'

Jay gave an ironical laugh. 'Princess, I thought you were dying for love of me.'

'I'll marry you and bear your child . . . children. I want the right to say when. Is that enough?'

'Enough for now. You're going to be a great wheeler-dealer.'

He lay down again, and though she rolled away from him across the wide bed he lifted her back. 'I want to hold you. It wouldn't be a deal otherwise. I know who you are. You're the sweetest little girl who used to stare up at me with great silvery, starry eyes. Nowadays, of course, those same eyes nearly blow me across a room.'

'I can't sleep like this,' she protested.

'Sure you can. You're going to be doing it for the rest of your life.'

Brett relaxed in amazement, her eyelids so heavy, it was a great effort not to close them with a sigh. Because Jay was who he was she was nearly accepting this incredible situation.

'Of course, we don't have to wait for a wedding if you don't want to?' He lifted her face and stared into her eyes.

'My wedding night will be my first time,' she told him. 'And probably not even then. I can't see myself loving you by then.'

'Ah, the lies you women tell!' Jay lifted her more comfortably back into his arm. 'Did I ever tell you, Brett, I loved my father.'

'I know, Jay.'

He nodded and relaxed his taut body. 'I suppose it's not unexpected for a little witch to know everything.'

CHAPTER THREE

A SOFT light fell into the room, piccaninny light when the pearlised sky was sheened with lemon. The pre-dawn breeze that fluttered around the bed was sweet and cool, causing little shivers to run along Brett's exposed skin. She made a movement of drowsy protest, then her eyes flew open as consciousness rushed into her brain.

She sat up in agitation, her heart leaping so violently she lifted a hand to her throat as though to keep it there. 'Dear God!' she whispered throbbingly. It was fantasy to be in bed with Jay; the fabric of her tell-tale dreams. She trembled in tingling shock and crossed her arms over her instantly yearning breasts. Her blood whipped into life and for an agonising instant she fought not to wake him with her lips against the clean chiselled curve of his mouth. He was as handsome as handsome, with a terrible power. His skin was very finely textured, with the colour of bronze. Hair, long thick eyelashes, brows, emphatically black. Darkness like that surely demanded dark eyes? One could scarcely absorb the shock of burning blue.

Such looks had made her, betrayed her. She had sold herself to him.

The ritual of mourning had ceased at the creek. An immense silence reigned in the short lull before the valley resounded with the heart-stopping songs of millions of birds. Brett felt as pent-up at dawn as she had ever felt the night before. What was the bargain? Jay would take her, control the fortune his father had left her, in exchange for a bitter victory. Marriage.

Her face crumpled and Brett twisted abruptly to get up. Heartache and confusion was all she had ever had from the Carradines. She thought she would get away, but an arm snaked out and drew her back with compelling force. She thrashed a little, but Jay rolled so that she was lying back against the pillows and he was leaning over her.

'Did I hear you cursing just a moment ago?'

'Did I wake you?'

'You could have done it better. With a kiss.'

'No kisses.' She stared up at him with her great luminous eyes.

'Then I'll take one.'

'Jay . . .' Her mouth trembled.

'Need I point out that I keep to my bargains? Incidentally, more than flesh and blood can stand.'

'I have to get out of here,' she muttered.

He bent his head. 'Who would have believed such a beautiful young enchantress could be so cold?'

With his mouth against hers the very air seemed to melt.

'Jay.' She put her hands against his shoulders, pushing with ineffectual strength.

'You're damned right,' he rolled away from her abruptly, 'if you're going to get out of here at all, you'd better go now.' He swung up and moved to the door, opening it and looking down into the long corridor. 'Can't see a soul.'

Brett slipped her robe over her nightgown and

lifted her hair over the neckline. 'Would you care if you did?'

'We could use ropes,' he mocked her. 'I could lower you down to the next floor.'

'*Are* we going riding?' she asked him.

'I have to clear my head.'His blue eyes were skimming her delicate face and body. 'If anyone asked me I could tell them you're just as beautiful first thing in the morning.'

'Whereas you have to shave.'

Jay ran a hand over his lean cheek. 'Hell's going to break loose when we announce our plans. You know that, don't you?'

'I'm used to a lot of fireworks.'

'Is there any possibility that you're going to want to get out of it?' His blue eyes seemed to burn into her like a brand.

'No.' She tilted her head to look at him. 'It's very important to me to get what my mother missed out on. You'll be a great man, Jay. Different from J.B.—more heart.'

'Anyway, we're quite fond of one another, aren't we?'

She saw the irony in his cool expression. 'My mother always told me I should be grateful to you, Jay.'

'What?' There was a searching frown on his face.

'Morton wasn't exactly nice to me, nor were any of your cousins. I could always see the contempt in their so civilised faces. I can remember once your knocking Morton down because he was teasing me.'

'You were just a little girl.'

'I remember.' She went past him to the door. 'You might have been a friend, but for what was between us. Pity moved you, Jay, and the same protective streak you had for your mother. What we have is a business arrangement that will allow us to guard all our interests.'

'Remember I want to sleep with you as well,' he pointed out drily. 'There are some things I can't do by myself.'

Brett saw no one on her way back to her room, and fifteen minutes later she was down at the stables where Jay had already saddled up the horses.

'We'll go east,' he said. 'Towards the rising sun.' There was a certain grimness to his expression as though he knew the next months would be very difficult to get through.

Brett sat her excited chestnut, admiring as she always did Jay's bearing in the saddle. He sat up tall, even after a hard day, never a slouch. There was a fascinating grace to his hard male body, something as superbly fit and disciplined as a top athlete and dancer combined.

The sun was beginning to mount into splendour, flaming on the horizon and now the birds were out in their hundreds; the great formations of budgerigars flashing vivid green as they put on their incredible displays over the flowering flats. This was one of the great sights of the Outback, the tens of thousands of beautiful little birds winging and wheeling against a dazzling blue sky. There had been just sufficient early spring rain for the vast flood plains to be softened by a miraculous carpet of wildflowers cropped by the horses as they galloped towards the ruined sandstone castles that marked the beginning of the hill country. To the aborigines

of the desert every strange natural feature told the
legend of a spirit ancestor, but many of the stories
were secret knowledge.

This early morning ride was balm to Brett's
grieving spirit as it offered comfort to Jay too. They
shared a deep abiding passion for this ancient
environment from its extremes of aridity to a
wonderland of wildflowers. Even the desert rivers
had many moods, flooding to run fifty miles wide,
then subsiding into chains of tranquil shallow pools.
In the history of the station, stockmen had been
drowned in flash floods and the homestead isolated
by a great inland sea. Diamond Valley was a world
apart, as bizarre and spectacular as the cratered
surface of some new planet.

They were riding parallel to the line of billabongs
when the wind wafted a soft woman-keening aloft.

'For God's sake, what's wrong now?' Jay reined
the black mare to a halt, turning his head and
listening intently. 'I don't like that at all.'

'Still for J.B., maybe?' Brett too felt a tightening
of her nerves. The aborigines had all kinds of
curious undulating cries and chants, but something
sounded different from the ritual mourning chants
of last night. The sound that now ran their blood
cold was more like the departure of a tribal
kinsman.

They rode down through the flowering bauhinias
and bright acacias to a stand of small ghost gums
standing white against the silver-green flash of lake.
Here, a handful of women were gathered around a
prone figure. One was at the figure's head, on guard,
and all of them turned to gaze at Jay and Brett as
they dismounted and began to walk soundlessly

across the thick grass tussocks to the shaded clearing.

'Oh, *no!*' exclaimed Brett.

'Wongin,' Jay agreed grimly. 'Stay there.'

While Brett remained at a respectful distance, Jay went to the head woman, who fell to her knees and began stroking the old man's head. 'He go now,' she muttered, sweeping Jay with her black liquid eyes. 'Wongin blood brother to King Carradine. You know all about that.'

Jay dropped to his knees, laying his own hand on the old aborigine's head as the women started up their low keening again. Like the night before, it was a form of respectful homage and an important stage in the transition of Wongin's spirit from this ancient watercourse to the Great Sky Country.

Jay remained for a few moments with bent head, even now after a lifetime with these people marvelling at their mystical powers. Wongin had chosen to die; there was no doubt about that. His surrendering up of earthly life had been symbolic of the deep bond between tribesman and white master. 'King' Carradine had gone to his hallowed place, and Wongin, who had given him life-long allegiance, had conducted his journey into the spirit world before electing to join him. It was as simple and extraordinary as that.

Brett sat down sharply in dire distress, and one of the women, a young lubra, came to her and plucking some wild herb that grew in the vicinity crushed the silvery-grey leaves between her brown fingers and held them under Brett's nose.

'There,' she whispered. 'There.'

The scent was sudden, delicious, neither flowery

nor citrus but incredibly aromatic. Brett inhaled it and gripped the emerald tussocks on either side of her. The plant's powerful fragrance cleared her head and something else beside. Within moments she felt better as though she had swallowed a tranquillising drug.

There was genuine concern and friendship in the young lubra's eyes, and Brett smiled at her and accepted a hand to get up. All aborigines had a profound kinship with nature and there were many, many wonderful herbalists and botanists among them. Jay's maternal grandfather, bitten by a desert death-adder, was commonly held to have been saved by some potion the station medicine man quickly brewed up. The white man had done everything to no avail; the brown man had survived desert living for more than forty thousand years.

The family were at breakfast when they returned to the homestead. Jay told them Wongin had passed over at dawn and, used to the ways of aborigines, they sadly accepted this extraordinary occurrence. All except the city-bred Elaine.

As Mrs Chase's prayerful little cry was dying on her lips, Elaine burst out bluntly, 'I don't know how you can accept all this superstition. The old guy was already three-quarters dead.'

'He wasn't at all!' Morton very nearly bellowed.

'Don't get your back up!' Elaine said in some amazement. 'May I please have more coffee?'

Morton got up to ring for more, placing a hand on Brett's shoulder as he passed. 'Already sitting at the family table?'

'Dear, dear Morton,' said Mrs Chase with a pained expression, 'I think you'll have to accept finally that Brett *is* family.'

'You realise we intend to contest the will?' Elaine drew in a hard breath.

'Who is *we*?' Jay raised his shocking blue eyes.

'Why, all of us, aren't we?' Elaine looked from old Mrs Chase at the head of the table back to Jay's dark, dominant face. 'We could make a very strong case.'

'Along what lines?'

Jay was reacting so oddly Elaine looked in some consternation at her husband. 'We all saw what she was doing to him—manipulating his mind.'

Jay gave a blistering laugh. 'No one, but *no one*, Elaine, will accept that image of J.B.'

'We can get something on her,' claimed Elaine.

'Would it help this conversation if I left?' Brett composedly folded her napkin and stood up.

'My dear, please have your breakfast,' Mrs Chase implored.

'Sit down, Brett,' Jay's voice cracked out. 'No one is going to hurt you. I hadn't planned to make any announcements now, but it might save Morton and Elaine a whole lot of time.' He switched his position so he was facing his grandmother, staring into her eyes and taking her hand. 'Grandma,' he said gravely, 'immediately the time's right—say six months from now—Brett and I are going to be married. It's what we both want, but you know ever since I was a little kid I've wanted, *needed*, your blessing.'

Morton cursed profoundly and Elaine jerked back so violently her chair scraped across the parqueted floor.

Mrs Chase said nothing, as though Jay was only

in the middle of his story. As indeed he was.

Brett left her chair and went to stand beside Jay, and he reached up his arm unexpectedly and looped it around her narrow waist.

'Brett and Jay,' murmured Mrs Chase, almost to herself.

'You're shocked, aren't you, Grandma?' Morton shouted.

'I hear you, Morton.'

'Hell, no wonder J.B. was afraid of Jay! I didn't realise he could outmanoeuvre the old master himself!'

'This won't happen, you hear me?' Elaine cried.' All the endless talk about you two—it could be true!'

'I have made it my business, Elaine, to establish that all the whispers were malicious lies,' the old lady said sharply, with a return to severity. 'I'll hear no more of it.'

'You know what they're doing, though, don't you, Grandma?' Morton implored. 'They're trying to cut me out.'

'Of what, my boy?' Mrs Chase, though she didn't relinquish the younger brother's hand, looked sympathetically on the other.

'No one would have to tell *you*,' Morton's drawling voice grew impassioned. 'Just as J.B. took Diamond Valley off Granddad, Jay wants to take everything off me. He wants to wield total power. All those fights with the old man! They're two of a kind.'

'How about talking a bit of sense?' Jay advised his brother shortly. 'What joy do you have in taking control? You don't even want Diamond Valley.'

'Who says?' Morton's throat was dry.

'You ought to teach your in-laws to keep their mouths shut '

'Aaah!' Mrs Chase gave an agonised little moan 'We must *never* let Diamond Valley go The pain that it caused me when your grandfather had to sell out was just bearable when I knew it would come back to you boys.'

'With Brett here, in the middle.' Elaine gave the younger girl a terrible glare. 'You know he wouldn't even look at you but for the way things turned out. Why, he's been seeing Kerri Whitman right up until a week ago. They had a private suite on the island. You saw her only yesterday. As far as *she's* concerned, Jay loves her. After all, she's from one of the old families, not an insignificant little no one!'

'Insignificant little no one?' A contemptuous smile crossed Jay's mouth. 'Brett could take her place anywhere, Elaine, and you know it. Not only is she beautiful, she's highly intelligent and accomplished. I consider these things far greater assets than coming from an old family such as the Whitmans. I don't intend to discuss *my* business, but I've never told Kerri I loved her, neither did we share a suite on the island. I didn't decide to marry Brett overnight—I've had it planned for a long, long time.'

'He could at that!' Morton turned his blond head to stare at his brother. 'There's no telling with Jay. He knew J.B. wouldn't leave Brett unprovided for. He might have even known just how well. The two of them could have planned it together.'

'There were no plans, Morton.' Brett looked at him with light-filled eyes. 'Never in my wildest dreams did I imagine Jay would want to marry me.'

'So how did you fall in love?' shrieked Elaine. 'Or doesn't *love* have anything to do with it?'

'*You* certainly don't,' Jay returned with icy arrogance. 'You overstep your place in this family, Elaine. You're my brother's wife. You're free to make a comment when your opinion is sought, otherwise keep out of it.'

'Are you going to let him speak to me like that, Morton?' Elaine asked awkwardly, an unbecoming flush on her high cheekbones.

'God, what do you want me to do? Let him break my neck?'

'I'd like to speak to you, Brett, when you're ready to talk to me,' Mrs Chase said. 'I know my grandson well enough to realise he permits nothing to get in his way. I'm not saying that he mightn't want you very badly, but you must show me what *you* want.'

Their talk didn't take place until late afternoon when Morton and Elaine took the jeep out on a long inspection of the property. Elaine was visibly subdued and Morton appeared to be in a state of shock.

'Sit down, Brett,' Mrs Chase said gently. 'You know I've always been fond of you so there's no need to be nervous. You're very young—twenty. You have no one—no woman relative outside of me so I want you to think of me as your honorary grandmother.'

'Were I ever so blessed.' Brett moved gracefully to sit opposite the old lady. 'What is it you would like to know?'

'Only one thing really,' Mrs Chase sighed. 'Do you love my grandson?'

A wave of emotion flowed over both women. The older disguised it through long habit, the younger reacted as if in pain. 'Do birds fly?'

'Would you like to tell me exactly, my dear?' For the first time Mrs Chase smiled.

'I can't remember when I didn't love him,' Brett confessed. 'I idolised him as a child, then as I grew up it went deeper—so deep I thought it was hidden.'

'And you've known Jay wanted to marry you for some time?'

I can't lie to her, Brett thought. To Morton, Elaine, anyone, but not to Mrs Chase. 'Jay asked me to marry him last night. I don't really know his reasons. Jay's no open book. He's a man who makes plans, so I expect my inheritance has a great deal to do with it. I think *he* thinks of it as Chase money. He's always had a thing about your side of the family that intensified with the years. He's always been determined to get his mother's money back. Even to this day his parents' failed marriage is an open wound. I don't think Jay holds marriage very sacred.'

'There's no question he's been very wary of coming into it,' Mrs Chase looked deeply reflective. 'I'm intensely anxious about this, Brett. I don't want you to get hurt—you've been hurt enough. It's my view that Jay has a deep attachment to you. You've shared so much. You've lived in the same house——'

'Neither of which has influenced Morton.'

'Morton isn't immune to you either. You're a very beautiful girl, Brett. You don't need me to tell you that.'

'Beauty may gain attention, but it doesn't turn a

lover into a husband,' said Brett quietly.

'It's worth stressing that J.B. didn't marry your mother for *Jay*. Whatever the clashes between them they were father and son, very much alike in lots of ways. Much as J.B. provoked conflict, he couldn't begin to cope with the idea of setting your mother up as mistress of Diamond Valley and stepmother to the boys. Jay, and Morton to a much lesser extent, was markedly affected by the whole tragedy. He was at the wrong stage of his emotional development to lose his mother the way he did. She had acquired a knight and Jay considered he had lost the battle. It says a great deal for his affection for you that he has always looked after you, no matter how high-handed it might have appeared at the time. Both of my grandsons have had to cope with a lifetime of frustrations, but now that's all over. It's inevitable that Jay will gain power and control. The differences between the two boys are great. I can't really see that Jay needs your voting power at all. Everyone within the corporation will look to him as the next chairman. He has always been more powerful, more aggressive, more dominant than Morton. He's perfected a very authoritarian manner, and compared with J.B. he's positively loved. J.B. liked people to fear him, but Jay likes to dominate through achievement. The one thing he cannot do is subdue you. What it seems to me is, you and Jay have arrived at some kind of resolution of the unhappy past.'

'I don't think he loves me,' Brett said poignantly.

'Then how can you go into this marriage, dear child?'

'Maybe I'm neurotic?' Brett suggested wryly.

'Not *you*, though we all have hang-ups, my dear. I suppose at your deepest level of thought you wish to avenge your mother?'

'I can't deny it,' said Brett. 'Maybe it's the ultimate symbolic gesture. At the same time I know I can make Jay happy if he'll only let me. My heart is exclusively his. I gave it up as a child. I suppose a psychiatrist would call it obsessive love—but Jay is such a romantic man. He's so vivid and vital, incapable of a mean action. J.B. had brilliant intellectual capacities, but he did a lot of terrible things. Jay, I know, makes a clear distinction between driving a hard bargain and being utterly pitiless. There's nothing in this world I want more than to be beside him. He doesn't just use the land to make money; he cherishes it like I do. For all J.B.'s dealings in stock and land, and how consummately shrewd they were, his personal fortune came before everything. He wasn't a great philanthropist like your own family. Chase money built hospitals and schools and endowed research institutes.'

'Well,' Mrs Chase sighed, 'if J.B. gave very little away he certainly died an exceedingly rich man. Diamond Valley in the old days was a very happy place. Of course so much changed after the Second World War. Very few of us, even the very rich, could afford to maintain the old Edwardian splendour. My own dear father employed fourteen gardeners. Needless to say he had a passion for gardening and hothouses and shade houses but my husband's family owned thousands of acres at one time, with a chain of stations running from the Gulf of Carpentaria to the markets in Adelaide. They built many magnificent houses, as you know, the centres of great pastoral communities, but two wars robbed them of the sons they desperately needed, and my own dear husband, though an exceptionally good man, lacked his forebears' legendary fire and genius. He was no match for J.B. He simply rode in one day as handsome as a dispossessed archangel and struck up a bargain. The bargain included my daughter. J.B. as a self-made man always had a hunger for position. I saw love in my daughter's eyes. I saw ambition in J.B.'s. I would not like to see history repeat itself.'

Whatever the truth, Brett thought, I have to face it. No matter how brutal that truth might be. It was impossible not to see the parallel.

Brett was dressing for dinner when Elaine came to her room, thin face tense, blue eyes glittering.

'Don't you think it's time you and I had a little talk?' she gritted.

Brett was suddenly very angry. For years she had endured Elaine's appalling arrogance; now she had withstood enough.

'How dare you come into my room like this!' she cried, seizing up a precious silver-backed brush as though she intended to fling it. 'There's no way I could go to yours and just force my way in. I'm not the helpless child I was, and this is now as much my house as yours—more, and I'd like you to leave.'

'I'll leave when I get some answers,' Elaine returned unpleasantly, and flounced into one of the moiré-upholstered armchairs. 'Don't play the heiress with me. Whatever good fortune has happened to you, you're still the housekeeper's daughter!'

'And what the devil are you, the scion of some noble family? Your grandfather made his money tinning sausages. Snobbery is not the democratic way,' retorted Brett.

'Most of us take it to our bosoms.'

'What do you mean, *most*? All you society layabouts?'

Elaine sprang up, eyes blazing, and slapped Brett across the cheek. 'You're a very rude girl—ill-bred. It's quite impossible for you to marry into this family.'

Brett saw her chance. She deplored physical violence but ended up choosing it. She bent swiftly and jerked the small silk Qum rug from beneath Elaine's booted feet. It seemed to her almost a blow below the belt, but she wasn't going to have the likes of Elaine slapping her face.

'You bitch!' screamed Elaine as she went down.

'Don't expect me to apologise.' Brett regarded the older girl contemptuously. 'If all the civility you can muster is slapping my face you can't expect I won't return the insult. What I do is no business of yours, nor of Morton's, unless it infringes on business. I know you've come here to tell me all about Kerri Whitman's affair with Jay. I know she's a friend of yours and I reject all your lies.'

'No lies!' Elaine, flushed with rage, struggled to her feet. 'You'll pay for that!' Incredibly her lip trembled. 'Don't think you can hide behind Jay.'

'I never have, so why would I start now? I've always had to take on opponents much bigger than myself.'

'You do realise, of course, that Jay is using you? You're supposed to be a clever girl, so try to be rational. On your own admission you never in your wildest dreams—wasn't it?—aspired to becoming

Jay's wife, yet immediately J.B. dies and leaves you equal beneficiary with his own sons, Jay proceeds to propose. We all know Jay. I can hardly afford to be too friendly. He's seeking absolute control—you know that, don't you? He's seized on your windfall to get it. Your combined clout will rob my husband of his rightful place as chairman of the Carradine Corporation.'

'I know nothing about high intrigue.' Brett turned away and dropped the silver brush on the dressing table. 'I do know Jay is J.B.'s logical successor. Morton, even if he is the elder, had no such ambitions until you succeeded in getting your claws into him. I realise your father and brothers are behind you. No doubt they regard it now as *their* money, or at the very least your children's inheritance. Isn't that the dynastic *modus operandi*? Empires have to be protected.'

'I see you have some grip on the situation,' Elaine said acidly. 'This must seem like the impossible dream for you, but go ahead with it and believe me, it will turn into a nightmare. He's got a showdown with Kerri to face. You don't spend a week with a man for nothing. I had a long conversation with her only yesterday, and Jay led her to believe he would marry her quite soon. Oh, Jay denied it with his customary arrogance, but I suspect you have your doubts. Only a fool wouldn't wonder why his proposal came out of the blue. Jay can think a whole strategy out in seconds. Don't worry, we all admire him, but he's not his father's son for nothing. Morton has nothing of J.B. Jay has too much.'

'Which makes him irresistible to me,' Brett feigned cynicism. 'As I'd like to point out, I cared a great deal for J.B. He was a hard man, a very hard man, but he offered me security and protection. I'm not glad he saw fit to raise me to the status of his own sons, but I am pleased in a sense to give it all back. I'm much too ignorant of big business to expect to take over some of the reins myself—not yet. But I've a good brain and I intend to learn. I promise you I won't remain too long in the dark. Jay isn't the only one good at decision making and making real use of unexpected opportunities. I chose Jay as much as he chose me. Our motives don't concern you, but if you're in any doubt that he's not attracted to me, you and Kerri Whitman can put that out of your minds. Jay knows exactly the kind of wife he wants. *Me*.'

'And while you're ticking off your attributes,' Elaine told her viciously, 'put balance of power at the top of your list. Jay's played the field in the past. He's a handsome, virile man and women chase him wherever he goes. He doesn't love you, so he won't be faithful. Thought of that? You'll be stuck here on Diamond Valley—always supposing you're fool enough to want to keep this great white elephant, and Jay will be jetting around. You're much too young at twenty to know it all. There's a dark side to Jay, and you're going to find out!'

CHAPTER FOUR

SOMEHOW Brett contrived to get through the following months. Diamond Valley was much too isolated to be a home base for either Jay or Morton, so they continued to live in Adelaide—Morton and Elaine in the Lodge, that was part of the original Chase estate; Jay in one of three pieds-à-terre he retained in the Southern capitals.

Brett remained on Diamond Valley, where she worked much too hard to be lonely. With a great deal of money put at her disposal she began refurbishing the house, consulting often with Jay's grandmother, not only as a mark of respect but for the old lady's excellent advice. They shared a classic eye and both wished to preserve the spirit of the great homestead. It was more a question of using what was to hand; an abundance of antique furniture and art works of all kinds, plus the treasures Brett unearthed; possessions overlooked for many long years. Walls were treated, curtains changed, sofas and armchairs re-covered, some of the guest rooms entirely re-done.

The only room Brett left severely alone was the old master bedroom suite with its sweeping views of the valley. It was as though she could hardly believe she and Jay might eventually sleep there. As it stood it was overpoweringly splendid, a relic of the Victorian era, but she knew how she could turn it into a luxurious, light and welcoming haven.

It remained unchanged, as did her curious relationship with Jay.

In the early months he had taken her on a long tour of the Carradine holdings. He treated her more as a trainee executive than a fiancée, though the formal announcement of their engagement was being withheld until a more appropriate time. The ring Jay had given her, a magnificent sapphire flanked by diamonds, dangled from a fine gold chain she wore around her neck. It was part of a matching set comprising necklace, pendant earrings, bracelet and ring that had been acquired at a Sotheby's auction some eighty years before. Brett knew the whole story. It had once belonged to an important English lady, and often as Brett fingered it she tried to visualise the woman who had first owned it. She must have had a fine and delicate hand. The band was small, but it fitted her fine-boned hand perfectly. Jay had not consulted her on the choice of ring. He had selected it himself from a considerable collection of family jewellery.

'The rest you'll get the day we're married,' he told her. 'You mightn't know it, but your eyes pick up colours like the dawn sky. I've seen them smoky blue, and lilac—even a tender green. You'll make a beautiful bride.'

Not a happy one. How *could* it be, when she wasn't much loved?

Mrs Chase approved the choice. 'I'm so glad Jay found it,' she said. 'The ring, of course, was much too small for me, but I did wear the necklace and earrings on a few occasions, mostly grand ones. My daughter never wore any of it to the best of my knowledge. We were considered beauties in our day, but we never had your heady quality, Brett. It makes for storms in life. That's why I worry.'

As Mrs Chase had predicted, there was no power struggle within the Corporation. Any coups had been pre-empted by the stunning news that Jay Carradine was to marry his father's little-known ward. For all Jay's formidable business genius, deep jealousies existed. Morton, since he had married into the Amery clan with its wide business interests, was being pushed along in his ambitions which were not normally excessive. He knew he could not compete with his younger brother at any level, and for much of his life this fact hadn't bothered him. In fact the two brothers, given the same harsh conditions, had been very close. The Amerys had changed all that. It was said Elaine Carradine had more aspirations in her little finger than her husband had in his whole six-foot-plus body. Unfortunately, when it was put to the vote, Carradine board members voted in a predictable way. None of them owed blind obedience to Amery interests and the Carradine Corporation was seen to be still a one-man show. John Carradine in his lifetime as head of his own organisation had exercised near-absolute control. Factions existed, but they had been held under restraint. Board members saw clearly that John Carradine Junior was the only man for the job. Furthermore, his soon-to-be bride was an important board member.

In this vein, Brett turned her attention to the study of economic corporations. She had always been an excellent student and now her major aim was to learn as much as she could about large-scale operations. She read widely from a pile of books an economics lecturer at her old university sent her, also all the literature she could find on the Carradine Corporation. She was unaware that she had made a very good impression on Carradine board members, many of whom thought as traditional chauvinists that she would be very easily controlled and manipulated. It seemed she had a brain, to be expected in a twenty-year-old man but an unexpected plus in a pretty girl when it wasn't really imperative.

Brett worked hard, on all things. Jay came and went. His attitude towards her could not even remotely have been termed 'loverlike'. Neither was it warmly affectionate as to family. It was strictly businesslike. She was a welcome addition to the Carradine Corporation and she was shaping up well. She received lots of impassive praise and active encouragement. She did not receive any more of the lovemaking that had awakened her body to sexual ecstasy. In all important respects they had made a business deal.

This didn't help her when the mail arrived, along with certain items forwarded by the interior design firm working with her on the refurbishing. A brief note from Jay informing her that he would be bringing guests for the long weekend seven in all—two personal letters for herself—girl friends from her university days—a stack of mail for Jack Moran, the station manager, and a padded post bag that had to be business because it bore her name and address on a white sticker.

She opened it first to get it over with, never expecting the sheaf of glossy photographs that spilled out. They were all of the same two people,

Jay and Kerri Whitman. Pretty monotonous, really. Jay and Morton were both crack polo players. One of the photos showed Jay leaning down from his polo pony receiving a congratulatory kiss from an excited and radiant Kerri. She appeared to be gripping him tight around the neck, no doubt in an excess of emotion. Others showed them enjoying leisure moments, on a yacht. Kerri was wearing a minuscule bikini that couldn't find a flaw in her long, lithe body. They were smiling into one another's eyes at a dinner table. Kerri was wearing a low-cut strapless dress and a wonderful-looking necklace, and her lips looked full and glossy. Dates were stamped on the backs of the photographs. The photographs purported to be recent. Brett put them away and didn't look at them again.

Jay and his party flew in on the following Friday afternoon. Brett wasn't surprised to see Kerri Whitman among their number, but she was surprised by the warmth and friendliness of Kerri's greeting.

'How lovely to see you, Brett!' Hazel eyes sparkled. 'Jay's been telling me all about your efforts at interior decoration. I can't wait to see them.' The words were certainly ambiguous. The smile seemed straightforward.

'Brett!' Jay compelled her to him, turning up her chin and staring into her eyes. Then he lowered his handsome dark head and lightly brushed her mouth.

The public image.

'I've missed you.' As soon as his lips left hers Brett gave him a slow, enchanting smile. It hinted of many things—all of them illusions.

Jay narrowed his eyes. 'Let me introduce David

Cooper,' he took hold of the arm of an attractive, grinning young man. 'I think you know everyone else. Dave is just back from a working tour overseas. He's a lawyer by profession. I'm trying to convince him to join our team.'

'Not *trying*, Jay,' David Cooper smiled, and then to Brett, 'this is one hell of a man you've got here, Brett—I may call you that?'

'Please.' Brett liked him at once. He had thick, glossy brown hair and humorous brown eyes. No hooded arrogance to David's open regard, and Brett found it thoroughly pleasing.

A moment later she was greeting Jay's other guests. People who had once virtually ignored her now sought her company. It had to be money.

'You'll be friends with me, won't you?' Kerri begged. 'I swear on my honour I'll try to cure myself of Jay.'

Brett smiled serenely. 'I'm so pleased there are no hard feelings, Kerri.'

The cruellest kind of training now stood her in good stead. She was a success with everyone at dinner. Jay wanted no shadowy figure at his side; he wanted a woman with a mind of her own and the ability to express it. It was fortunate she was highly intelligent and had been given the opportunity to receive an excellent education. The conversation ranged over a wide sphere of interests, and though Kerri Whitman did her level best to engineer a few bright-eyed put-downs, it was very obvious who was the more intelligent, the more informed of the two.

Afterwards David asked her to stroll with him in the garden. He had scarcely taken his eyes off her at dinner, but whether because of her looks or conversation Brett didn't know.

'How poised you are for such a young woman,' he complimented her warmly. 'Why, I could give you eight or nine years, and I feel a schoolboy by comparison.'

'I think you're being very kind to me, David.'

He lightly took her elbow and guided her down the wide, shallow flight of steps. 'I'd heard of you, naturally, but I didn't *see* you the way you are.'

Brett could well imagine. 'I insist you tell me what you heard?' she countered lightly.

Darkness covered David's faint flush. 'Why, that you were as beautiful as night. You were John Carradine's ward. Young—no more.'

'Suitable?'

'I think Jay is very much to be congratulated,' David responded gallantly. 'I think you're the perfect match for him.'

'May I ask why?' Brett lifted her lovely face. She was wearing her dark cloud of hair in a loose roll to complement the almost Grecian line of her white dinner dress, and it emphasised the purity of her features. Her voice matched her looks.

David was enchanted. 'For one,' he said ardently, 'Jay deserves the best. Enormous success has come to him very early and it's not easy being the man at the top. He holds the reins of power. From what I've seen, power can be dehumanising. You're a caring, compassionate young woman. I've been listening to you at dinner, and I like your views, the tolerance of your attitudes. Obviously you have a good brain and you intend to use it to the full. Speaking as a male, I think women have been held back too long. You'll be good for Jay, good for the Corporation. I think women bring a saner approach to business. You'll act as a fine balance. The whole character of the Carradine Corportation was moulded and established by Jay's father. It's generally accepted that he was an autocrat solely responsible for company decisions and policy. Jay's a man who looks for solutions when Corporation interests conflict with the interests of particular individuals, or even the ecology.'

'I know what you mean.' Brett nodded her head. 'Jay convinced the board to take a stand with the conservationists. There'll be no more clearing of the rainforest on Carradine holdings. That wouldn't have happened in J.B.'s day. Jay cares deeply about the land—that's the Chase heritage. It often seems strange to me that Morton, who resembles so strongly the Chase side of the family, should have little feel for his home and this extraordinary environment. He considers the homestead a white elephant. It certainly costs a great deal to maintain.'

'It's absolutely splendid!' David burst out rapturously, turning to look back at the brilliantly lit mansion. 'The first time I've been here, as you know. It's quite, quite breathtaking to come on in what could be a great wild-life sanctuary. It's positively unique!'

'Well—unique to this part of the world,' agreed Brett. 'The old squatocracy was the equivalent of the British aristocracy. Many a second son made a great fortune here, so he built the kind of house he was used to. The homestead has the same importance as the Home Country's castle. It was possible for certain men, the great cattle kings like Kidson and Tyson, to build up vast estates the size of

England and more. Diamond Valley homestead is an excellent example of the golden years. It's still in the hands of the same family and it still retains its original glory.'

'Another thing I was wanting to compliment you on,' David told her. 'Twenty years hardly seems enough for you to have learned so much. The refurbishing—isn't that what you call it?—is positively brilliant. I can tell you the whole place has knocked me absolutely flat!'

'I would never have done so well but for Mrs Chase.'

'Ah yes, a marvellous lady! Full of vigour.'

'She spent a very long time here. To me it's still filled with her presence. It was she who lavished so much loving care on the home gardens,' Brett told him.

'Extraordinary!' David was still reaching for superlatives. 'By far the most striking aspect of it is the enormous size of the plants. One would have thought it would be very difficult indeed to grow anything in a desert environment, but all this is absolutely beautiful!' He waved a hand over the richness and extent of the gardens. 'One wonders how so much wealth fell into the hands of the one family.'

'*Two* families,' Brett corrected gently. 'Chase and Carradine, and it didn't just *fall*. There was a lot of agony mixed up with the exultation. You would only have to visit the station cemetery. Before the days of the Flying Doctor Service the Outback was no place to be if anything went wrong.'

'I can imagine,' David retorted. They were walking along a softly lit corridor of cypresses and he turned quickly to peer down at her. 'For all its magnificence, Brett, you don't find it a lonely prison?'

Her silver eyes seemed to flash. *'Never!'* she said fervently. 'Diamond Valley is no prison to me. It's my protection.'

'A strange word, surely?' David found himself countering. 'Why would a beautiful, clever girl like yourself wish to hide?'

'Did I say *hide*?' She gave him an enigmatic smile.

'Damn it, I'm sorry. The fact of the matter, Brett, is you're the sort of girl one gets awfully emotional about. I've only just met you and I'm under your spell. Are you quite sure you're mortal?'

'If you pinch me I'll pretend it doesn't hurt.'

'Why have you been here all these months?' David's brown eyes darkened.

'You mean I shouldn't sit back and let certain things happen?' Brett asked almost bluntly.

'Jay doesn't give a damn about Kerri Whitman.' David immediately betrayed his knowledge of the situation. 'I only meant I would have thought Jay would want you by his side. I know I couldn't bear to leave you out of my sight were you my fiancée.'

'And how would the refurbishing have been done?' Brett moved on, the top of her head reaching David's shoulder. 'No, David, it suits us both to get things done. We have the rest of our lives.'

'And Jay is getting a jewel.'

When they came in some fifteen minutes later, David was looking both exhilarated and excited. Brett had promised to take him out riding first thing in the morning, and such is the mass of contradictions human beings are, as much as he admired and respected Jay and indeed was thrilled at the prospect of joining the Carradine Corporation, he was allowing himself the outrageous hope that Brett might see him as a second choice. Love at first sight wasn't particularly uncommon, though circumstances made people hold their feelings in a suspended state. Brett was Carradine's fiancée; a powerful deterrent, yet already David was allowing himself to be impelled towards danger.

Kerri, sitting on the sofa, seized on David's giveaway expression. She lifted her head to Jay and said something that brought a hawklike watchfulness to his lean, handsome face. Brett in her white gown was the picture of patrician elegance. She was smiling, a real smile that reached her dazzling eyes, but no more. There was a visible aura of rapport between them, but when Kerri swung about to gauge Jay's expression all she received was a clear view of his arrogant profile.

The soft rap on her door brought Brett to attention. She had been sitting at her dressing table brushing out her hair preparatory to going to bed. Her head was a kaleidoscope of thoughts and for one ghastly moment she thought it might be Kerri. Kerri, who appeared to be so friendly, was a powerful enemy— Brett knew that, as she was meant to know. Kerri was playing secret games. The Whitmans, winners for so long, wouldn't sit still and lose everything now. If there was a way to break up this extraordinary engagement they would call all their formidable resources into play. The photographs were only the start.

Brett was clasping her hairbrush so tightly her knuckles showed white. She was determined to be proud and brave—she had no other choice—but her heart was thumping uncomfortably. A session with Kerri Whitman was the last thing she wanted. Nevertheless she swallowed hard and went to the door, the hem of her long aqua peignoir just brushing the floor. She was glad now that she could afford such glamorous nightwear. It shouldn't, but it did make her feel more sure of herself.

Instead of Kerri, Jay was standing outside the door, one hand resting against the jamb in an attitude of mild impatience.

'My dear Marisa!' He gave her a sweeping bow.

'Yes, Jay?'

His blue eyes were amused, searching. 'You're obviously deeply surprised to find your fiancé outside your bedroom door.'

'Actually, yes,' she returned coolly. 'I thought we shook hands an hour ago.'

'My dear, I'm sure I kissed your cheek.'

'And believe me, I'm very grateful.'

'May I come in?' he asked airily, one black eyebrow lifting at the acerbity of their exchange.

'Oh, do.' Brett turned away from his unsettling regard. 'It will give us a chance to talk over the last months.'

'I must say I adore that nightgown and robe. It's simply gorgeous. You're not expecting a visitor, surely?'

'One can't be certain of anything in this house.' Brett slid into an armchair and indicated the one opposite her with her hand.

'You did very well tonight.' Jay didn't sit but allowed his gaze to move around the room. 'I knew you were boning up, of course, but I had no idea how intensively. You're a very bright girl.'

'I'm delirious with your praise!' she said drily.

He swung his head back and something in his eyes silenced her. 'Don't complicate things, will you?'

'It would be a bonus if you'd tell me what you mean.'

'Have you any idea how much Dave wants to come and work for us?'

'David?' She frowned. 'What has David to do with this?'

'Dave is a man like any other. He can be seduced by a pair of sparkling eyes. You know how the song goes.'

Brett gritted her small white teeth and pushed up out of her chair. 'If this is an exhibition of jealousy, Jay, it's extremely unsuccessful.'

'It's Dave I'm concerned about,' he remarked drily. 'It would be a mistake to give him the lightest encouragement. He's a man I don't care to lose.'

'You don't need to drop *your* admirers, of course?' Colour swam into her cheeks. 'Engagements shouldn't take all the fun out of life.'

Jay didn't answer that at all. He even acted as though she hadn't spoken. 'Don't think I'm blaming you, Brett,' he drawled pleasantly. 'I know you can't help this fascination thing—it came with you at birth. Put simply, I don't want to risk losing Dave. For his sake, if not mine, nip his infatuation in the bud. You know perfectly well nothing can come of it. All that *will* happen is a ruined career.'

'I don't believe this,' she said slowly. 'I thought you'd be only too pleased to see me getting on with your friends, the people you bring here.'

'I don't want you to seduce them,' Jay said brutally. 'You're gifted that way.'

'Just who have I seduced in all these years?' she asked tightly, unaware that anger was heightening her beauty. 'How can you accuse me of such a thing?'

'Forget the dramatics, Brett,' he advised in a clipped voice. 'I've already said I know it's not really your fault. I just want to get this thing straight. Dave is attracted to you——'

'I don't——'

He held up his hand. 'Agreed?'

'I'm too confused to tell,' she sighed.

His laugh made her nape tingle. 'Do you think no one noticed you when you came in from your walk?'

'Oh, God, Jay!' She put up her hands and pushed her fingers through her dark cloud of hair. 'This is crazy! The reason I went with David was to please you. I like him, certainly, but I never considered even the mildest flirtation for one minute. I'm not looking for affairs; I'm not even looking for love. I've learned enough to know that it's in very short supply.'

'So it is!' Jay shrugged his wide shoulders, the very picture of arrogant self-sufficiency. 'You needn't look like that either. I *know* you, Brett. You're no different now from that heartbroken little girl. You conceal the intensity of your feelings under that swan-like disdain.'

'You're devastating when you're kind!'

He levelled his brilliant blue eyes at her, as

intimidating in their fashion as a loaded gun. 'Dave is fast losing his habitual good sense. No artifices are necessary with you, but that was a bravura performance tonight—the princess locked away in the enchanted wilds. Dave's reaction was immediate and passionate—I should know. You told him you'd take him out riding in the morning?'

'And what if I did?' Brett's dark hair framed her face, that haunting face now filled with emotion.

'I'll come with you, that's all.' The smile on his handsome mouth left no trace in his eyes. 'You *are* my fiancée. You can't expect me to take too kindly to Dave's involvement—or anyone else's, for that matter. I've never read a signal wrongly in my life. Dave thinks because I've kept you here he's freer in some way, but he couldn't be more wrong!' He looked at her long and mockingly, more handsome than the devil.

'I could change my mind,' she challenged him, her nerves stretching as they always did at the sight of his lean, lithe elegance.

'Not you, Brett.' His brilliant gaze returned hers. 'We're two of a kind. Both of us know how to survive hostile environments. Both of us *should* be emotionally burnt out. I want no other woman but you. You suit me very well.'

She moved closer so that he was inches from her, searching his eyes as if to penetrate the layers of concealment that masked his heart.

Ice turned to fire, anger to abrupt passion.

Jay took her nerveless wrist and drew her hard against his strong, sleek body. 'What are you, Brett, my Nemesis? Goddess of retribution?'

'Kiss me,' she said strangely—not a pleading but

an affirmation of her power.

'I'll let nothing destroy me. Not even you.'

'Kiss me, Jay.' The stillness of her expression did not alter, but her eyes grew enormous, shimmering like ice crystals.

'You'd like to bring me down, wouldn't you? Revenge a childhood filled with little humiliations.'

'You've always been in my deepest fantasies,' she said quietly.

'Did you think I didn't know what was happening to you?' He lifted a hand and grasped her by the hair. 'You talk of rape. There was never a question of rape between you and me. In the end it would have been impossible for you not to give yourself to me. I'm looking into your eyes, Brett.'

'They have secrets, just like yours. Is it possible you're a little frightened of me?' She was speaking softly, slowly, as though she sought to put him in a trance.

'So frightened I've stayed away.' He began to twine her silken hair around his hand. 'Dave couldn't take his eyes off you at dinner. You'd only have to snap your fingers and the poor devil would throw up a brilliant career. Your beauty doesn't end at admiration. It's black magic. Not a shadow show, the real thing.'

'So why don't you kiss me?' she whispered.

His reaction was sizzling. His grip so powerful it almost cut off her breath. She was bent backwards over his arm while the heat that was in him scorched her mouth and her body. Passion rose in a great wave.

She should have screamed for the bitterness.

'Jay,' she whimpered against his violent kiss,

'you're cracking my bones!'

His hands travelled over her. She knew from their strength and authority what could lie ahead of her. There was a whole world of sensuality hidden behind her marriage vows.

The aqua peignoir fanned to the floor. It was as though he had to get nearer to her than the glistening film of satin. She was faintly conscious that she was moaning, turning her head as he drew his mouth along her throat.

He was her everything. *Everything*. Yet words of endearment were lodged in her throat. Love. Obsession. Maybe obsession was the better word for it.

He lifted her and turned with awful slowness towards the bed. His jaw was clenched and there was a primitive flare to his finely cut nostrils. The image of a conqueror leaped into her mind. His eyes were brilliant, the only living things in a golden, taut mask.

She came down on the cloud bed with a sense of falling through space. The lace strap of her nightgown had fallen off her shoulder and her small, high breasts were almost exposed to his view—dazzling white skin, wonderful rosy peaks.

She turned her head to look up at him, but he was still staring down at her with the same hard and consummate mastery. What was she anyway but a possession to be subjugated?

Unless she could foil him.

She slid across to the other side of the bed and stood back against the wall. A small bronze figure of a dancer was always on her bedside table, and she seized it up and held it like a threat.

'It would be terrible to harm you, Jay,' she warned.

Incredibly he smiled. 'Are you aware what you look like? I don't want to rob you of any confidence, but I could smother you in a second.'

'Is that what you *want* to do?'

'What I want to do is put my brand on your flesh. You tend to revert to the wild.'

'Dominion over a woman's body isn't dominion over her heart.'

'I know that, Brett,' he returned sombrely, and turned away from her as though weary of the conquest.

She came away from her place of retreat beside the waterfall of silk curtain and moved towards the bedside table. How was it possible to feel wounded yet desperate for more? What was she, a masochist? Why was there excitement in wishing Jay would subdue her? She wanted him, that was why. She wanted him so much she was exhausted with the force of it. Desire was like tongues of fire licking at her flesh. Jay represented all she had ever really wanted in life. Jay was her past and her future, but where was love?

In the end he took the exquisite little figurine from her, placing it gently on the bedside table. He moved, as she well knew, as swiftly as the wind. She stood before him, incapable of movement, and all at once he turned into the Jay of her childhood: champion of weeping little girls.

'Come here,' he said quietly, his high-mettled face, so stormy at times, filled with a rare empathy.

What then?

In the next second he lifted her and put her down

across his knees. 'Honest to God, Brett, sometimes you wring my heart! You've taken so much. We *both* have, yet we can't abandon the old grievances. Sometimes I think we even fight to hold on to them.'

'Why did you kiss me so savagely?' Despite herself she took comfort from his strong body, leaning back so that her dark head was against his shoulder.

'I can't help kissing you savagely,' he returned crisply. 'Where *you're* concerned I am a savage. Fighting me is like slamming a knife into my heart.'

She rose up swiftly, staring into his eyes. '*What* did you say?'

'So you can start carving it up?'

'I want truth between us, Jay.'

'Then supposing *you* start?' There was a faint bite to his voice as though there was no room for lies.

Brett's eyes glowed in her face. Her cheekbones were shadowed with soft colour. 'I've always wanted to be honest with you, Jay, but I never have.'

'I don't think you especially like how you feel.'

'Feel about you?'

'I don't mind if we talk all night. I think I have to kiss you hard to tranquillise you.'

She sighed deeply and leaned back against him. 'You shouldn't try to torment me with Kerri Whitman.'

'Don't be dumb,' he said shortly. 'It doesn't suit you.'

'Really?' Her temper matched his in less than a second. 'If you promise not to be embarrassed I'd like to show you something.'

'I think you'd better put your robe on, then.' His eyes burned over her shoulders and breasts, the graceful line of thigh and slender legs.

'Fine.' She moved off his knee and picked her peignoir up.

'In the meantime I should take a running jump into a cold shower,' said Jay drily.

'You stay there. You won't need a shower when this is over.'

'Marisa, I'm shocked!'

'I mean it.' She was angered by his mockery.

'All right, I'll just sit here and admire the femininity of your room. How come you haven't started on the master suite yet?'

Brett shook her head. 'I'm going to stipulate on this famous contract that we're to enjoy separate rooms.'

'What makes you think I would ever agree to that?' he asked lazily.

Brett took the large yellow envelope out of her bureau and pushed the drawer back. 'Not to mention accommodation for lovers.'

'Any lovers *you* might decide to take will be quickly buried. God, I damn near threw poor old Dave out of the house.'

She stopped before him and passed him the padded envelope.

He sat forward, his expression sharp. 'What *is* this, Marisa?'

'Guilty already?'

He glanced up at her with narrowed eyes. 'There's nothing you like more than a bit of mystery. I guess in another time I would have had to rescue you from burning.'

'Nobody ever stops to put a label on a man. Some people might call *you* a devil.'

'A devil by any other name.' Jay drew the photographs out slowly, not a trace of response in his face. 'Don't they have one of us in bed?'

'Did you want one of you in bed?'

'I get more out of just looking at you. This isn't a crime, is it, Marisa? Not a real crime. I see a man and a woman. Incidentally, one of these is years ago.'

'There are dates on the back.'

He leaned back and threw the phtographs into the fireplace. 'That's my response to these. They're just a bunch of you-know-what, intended to hurt you. I'm so glad they failed.'

'Well—I guess there are more. I'll probably get the one of the two of you in bed yet.'

'So what?' His blue eyes flared. 'Sleeping around is common these days. I would have made love to lots of girls—you know that. *You* were a child. Maybe I didn't love 'em, but that was all right in their book. All of them I still count among my friends. Most of them are happily married, for that matter.'

Brett nodded, aware that what he was saying was perfectly true. Women had chased Jay for years. *That* was magic, if you like. 'And what about Kerri?'

'Kerri can eat her heart out.'

'Elaine said you got around to talking marriage,' she said.

'And what do *you* think?'

'As a matter of fact I think I'd be very surprised.'

'Well then, Marisa,' Jay returned coolly, 'you know me better than you think.'

CHAPTER FIVE

BRETT rose next morning with every intention of doing what Jay told her. Perhaps David had been a little more attentive than necessary, but she was still surprised by Jay's reaction. She had merely been pleasant to a personable young man, but if it was going to jeopardise David's position in any way she would have to be very careful and controlled in her manner. Kerri Whitman would just love to stir up a little trouble!

She stood in the middle of her bedroom and surveyed her slender figure. Her cotton shirt and jodhpurs looked neat and businesslike, her riding boots had a commendable shine to them. She was a small girl, but no one could deny she was a fine rider. Her deep love of horses went back as far as she could remember; in fact during her lonely childhood horses had been the source of her greatest pleasure. On a great station like Diamond Valley it would have been unthinkable for her not to ride, and even her mother's tragic accident, terrible though it had been for her, could not change her affinity with these miraculous creatures. J.B. had been fascinated by her trick of singing to a favourite mount, and Brett had always told him it was a song of joy. Riding released all her tensions, and the trails on Diamond Valley were limitless.

'You look beautiful this morning, Brett,' murmured David as soon as he saw her.

'David, you mustn't flatter me too much,' she responded lightly, thinking perhaps Jay hadn't been exaggerating after all.

'Not flattery, Brett, the simple truth.' His brown eyes warmed. 'This is a first for me, you know. I've never been out on an early morning ride in my life.'

'But you *can* ride?'

Last night he had told her he could. Perhaps he had been joking.

'Put it this way, I can stay on providing I have a tame beast.'

'Ah well,' Brett couldn't help smiling at him, 'we have horses that understand every kind of rider. I talk to the lot of them.'

'Do you really?'

'Not only that, they talk back to me. Some of them won't shut up.'

'You really do look super in that gear,' David told her. 'I could literally worship at your booted feet.'

'By the way,' she turned her dark head, 'Jay is coming along with us.'

He went a little pink. 'I was afraid he might.'

'*David!*' She opened her large eyes.

'Is it too terrible to want you to myself?'

'You understand I'm engaged,' warned Brett.

'Jay has to be the luckiest guy in the world.' He held the door open for her as they walked through to the morning room. The intention was to have a quick cup of tea and delay breakfast until after their ride. Early mornings were superb. The air was so pure, and the vast plains and the desert fringe responded sublimely as the direction of the light varied. The intensity of colour was remarkable— the dramatic ochres, orange, yellow, chocolate

brown, the glowing blood red of the sand dunes, the
great purple chasms; it was this that gave Diamond
Valley its unique character. Brett was looking
forward to initiating another, sympathetic human
being into all this peace and beauty.

Kerri Whitman and Jocelyn Nolan, wife of one
of the Corporation's top executives, were already
seated at the large circular table enjoying a really
lavish breakfast. Both of them were pencil-slim, but
one of the great rewards of staying at the homestead
was to eat everything that was put on. Very few
guests ever stuck to their normal programmes, and
Brett had long since found she had to go sparingly
on the delectable breakfast bakery that issued from
Mrs Martin's kitchen. The brioches and croissants
in particular simply melted in the mouth.

'Oh, there you are!' Kerri called gaily. 'Come on
and sit down. Why not sit beside me, David? I'm
sure you're just dying to make inroads on all this
delicious food. I'll have to starve for a week, but it's
worth it!'

David and Brett smiled and said their good
mornings, and Brett explained that they only had
time for a cup of tea.

'And perhaps one of those golden little rolls.'
David too seemed distracted by the sumptuous
morning spread.

'Have you seen Jay?' asked Brett, walking to the
large bay window and looking out. 'He's coming
riding with us.'

'*Was* coming riding, dear,' Kerri amended. 'The
manager was up here a while ago and carried him
off—something about the sale of some Drought-
masters. He told me to tell you to go on. He'll

probably be with Moran for some time.'

David brightened as if he had been touched by the sun. 'That's it then,' he downed his cup of tea. 'Is this not a beautiful day?'

'Sure is, Dave,' Kerri agreed laconically. 'Be good.'

There was always a man at the stables, and it was he who saddled up a quiet gelding for David.

'Gosh, you're not going to ride *that*!' he exclaimed as Brett accepted a leg-up on to her beautiful, dancing mare.

Brett's silver eyes were glowing. 'Say hello to Rain Dancer.' The mare lifted, then shook her finely chiselled head, her big bold eyes showing her generous and animated temperament.

David, who didn't understand the display of excitability, saw it as a threat to the petite Brett.

'Hi there, Rain Dancer,' he called a shade apprehensively. 'Sure she isn't a bit too big for you?'

'Miss Brett can ride anythin',' the aboriginal hand grinned. 'It's you that's got to watch yourself, mister!'

While Rain Dancer was raring to go, the gelding's instinct was to walk back into the stables. Brett leaned over and gave it the slightest tap on the flank and it responded immediately.

They moved off.

It was possibly the most enjoyable morning Brett had experienced for months. David was quite content to sit his horse while she gave Rain Dancer periodic bursts of galloping. It was too much to expect either of them to keep to David's sedate pace, but for the most part they rode along companionably, side by side.

It was coming on to the Wet in the tropical North of the continent and they had been experiencing short downpours like mini-storms in the early mornings and around sunset. As a consequence the limitless flats were covered with mile upon mile of mulla-mullas, waving like the pussytails the desert dwellers called them, pink parakeelya, poppies, lilies, desert nightshades, annual saltbush and bluebush, the firebush cassia and the blinding mantle of white and gold paper daisies.

'It beats me how they call this a desert!' Brett exclaimed. 'The flowers go on for ever!'

'You're seeing the land in its time of glory. When rain falls, even a passing shower, the living desert springs to life. The seeds of these wildflowers are wonderful creations—they only need a drop of water to germinate. Later, in summer when the big heat is on, all these endless miles of wildflowers will fade and die. That's if the North doesn't flood from cyclones or heavy monsoonal rain. Then the Channel Country goes under. We've been cut off on plenty of occasions. All this, for instance, would be under water. People call it the Dead Heart, and it can be, but after rain or flood it's Nature's most incredible garden.'

David shielded his eyes from the dazzling glare of the paper daisies. 'At first glance from the plane, I thought how could anyone live out here, no matter how grand the homestead. It's so vast and lonely. That's the first impression. The isolation, I felt, would be too much for me. It's almost like living on your own planet. But this ... *grandeur* lifts my heart.'

Brett was delighted with his sincere appreciation.

'Have you seen the Centre, Ayers Rock, the Olgas? Uluru and Katajuta, the aboriginals call them.'

'Actually, though I've been all round the world and in every major city of my own country, this is my first visit to our great Outback, and it's affecting me profoundly,' David told her. 'Without realising it I have the most extraordinary place on earth at my own back door.'

'I suppose that would have to apply to the oldest continent on earth. By the same token we have enormous wilderness areas, great natural landscapes in a world where the wilderness has all but disappeared. I'm so glad you're finding all this special, David. I'm quite passionate about Diamond Valley.'

Brett's voice was low, vibrant, thrilling, and David looked at her with an almost poignant longing. It seemed to him he had never met such a girl in his life. Even the way she rode, free like the wind, excited him. She looked as delicate as a white camellia, yet she abandoned herself to the great outdoors. It was wildly unsettling.

A fine herd of shorthorns was luxuriating in the rich pastures, and Brett allowed David to inspect them before taking him down to the serpentine creek. The pebbles on the shore shone white and the whole area was a glowing canvas of rose-pink and green. Even the graceful gums were reflected in the mirror-still dark green water.

'This is fantastic!' David breathed. 'Wouldn't it be just perfect for a swim?'

'We really should go back,' Brett smiled at him. 'I can smell rain on the breeze.'

'You can?' He looked up at the peacock sky in

astonishment. He had missed the mauve clouds on the horizon.

The rain came down before they gained shelter, but neither seemed to care. It was, in fact, wonderfully refreshing, and Rain Dancer, true to her name, began to react to a good soak, going into an extravagant routine not unlike the haute école of the famous Lippizaners of the Spanish Riding School.

David was entranced. He had never had such an experience in all his city-bred life. The rain was wonderful. The horses were wonderful. The whole Valley was fantastic, but most of all, the girl.

They were laughing helplessly when they arrived back at the stables. The attendant had disappeared for a moment and David quickly dismounted and went to Brett.

'Here, let me help you. Honestly, you're soaked to the skin!' He had seen plenty of girls in the rain. Very few of them actually glowed like a flower.

Brett put her hands to her glistening head, then removed her feet from the stirrups, unaware that David was looking up at her as though she was the goddess of the hunt. 'Needless to say, it's all over. The showers are short and sweet.' She needed no help to dismount herself, but David obviously thought she did.

She slid down, and with her back against the mare David suddenly gripped her shoulders. He was on the point of kissing her; she knew it. She liked him so much she was shaken to discover he had developed such feeling for her so early and so unwisely.

'David——' she began.

His sun-browned face, his glossy head was poised over hers. Her expression was one of a supplicant.

'So *there* you are!' a familiar voice called ringingly.

David dropped his hands at once and Brett froze. Neither of them had heard footsteps in the courtyard, yet here were Jay and Kerri, dressed for riding.

'You obviously didn't wait for us,' Kerri accused them with mock grievance. 'Jay, do you really think you should allow your fiancée to go riding with attractive young men?'

Jay's brilliant blue eyes moved abruptly from David to Brett. His face wore an expression Brett knew well; a glittery arrogance that didn't bode well for David. For either of them, for that matter.

Brett didn't wait for his answer; she rushed to her own defence. 'You were the one who told us not to wait, Kerri,' she said decisively.

'Not *me*, darling.' Kerri laughed goodnaturedly. 'I was only fooling, you know. Jay knows he has nothing to be jealous about.'

David jerked up his head. 'Is this some kind of joke? Brett asked you where Jay was and you said he'd gone off with the station manager.'

'So I did!' Kerri responded wide-eyed. 'Hey, don't let's make an issue of this. If you didn't want to wait, you didn't want to wait.'

'You told us to *go*, Kerri,' David replied sternly.

'Shouldn't you two get out of those wet clothes?' Jay intervened. 'Whatever you *thought* Kerri said, I did intend for us all to go out together. No matter. Breakfast is waiting.'

'What about that Kerri?' muttered David as they

walked back to the house. 'She turned the tables on us, and it had to be deliberate.'

'I'm used to troublemakers,' Brett said briskly. 'I take them in my stride.'

'Jay looked kinda intimidating.'

'It comes easily to him.' Brett flicked a smoky look into his face, then looked away. 'You want to join the Corporation, don't you, David?'

'Obviously—that's why I'm here.'

'Perhaps it might be better——'

'If I didn't appear to enjoy your company so much?'

'I have enemies, David,' Brett warned him.

'I think you'd better include Kerri Whitman among those people,' David went on. 'I suppose you can't expect her to be fond of you. There was a time when Jay was going to marry her, wasn't there?'

'That rumour was put about,' she agreed.

'A lot of people heard it. I'm only back from overseas and *I* heard it. Wait a little minute, Brett.' He caught her arm. 'Normally I hate gossip, but I think it's obvious that I really like you. Be on your guard.'

'Can't you at least warn me from whom?'

'Has it ever occurred to you that Morton is very jealous of his brother?'

'Not right now, David. We have to change.' Brett walked on. 'I grew up here, you know. I know Jay *and* Morton as if they were my own family. Morton was never jealous of his brother until he married and his wife and her family convinced him he ought to be. Morton isn't as sure of himself as he appears to be. He and Jay had the same upbringing, and believe me, they're very close. If and when it really comes to it, blood will tell. Morton may be manoeuvred into any number of little skirmishes, but no one on this earth is going to make him raise his hand against his brother. Morton *loves* Jay. He doesn't hate him. But he could be persuaded to hate *me*.'

Some of their guests were still seated over breakfast when Brett and David eventually made their way back to the morning room. Brett, who believed in taking the bit between her teeth, looked across at Jocelyn Nolan. Mrs Nolan was keeping her husband company while he enjoyed a late, leisurely breakfast.

'We missed Jay,' Brett told her conversationally. 'Didn't Kerri tell us to go ahead?'

'Why, I believe she said to stay.'

'Oh, surely not,' intervened David, trying not to sound contemptuous.

'Well, I thought so,' Jocelyn Nolan replied apologetically. 'Excuse me, won't you? I have to get my sunglasses. I've never experienced such quality of light!'

'I've a feeling dear Kerri has something on Mrs Nolan,' David said later. 'She didn't want to lie, but she had to.'

If Kerri was feeling at all malevolent she managed to hide it well. For an outsider it would have been easy to believe she was taking this engagement very well. Her manner with Jay was that of a lifetime good friend spiced with the inevitable man-woman banter. She was provocative, certainly, but it was an integral part of her nature. Towards Brett she was friendly, albeit in a gently patronising way—something that might be

expected of an experienced sophisticate in her
dealings with a girl barely out of the classroom.
Occasionally Kerri was downright indulgent, giving the impression that Brett needed all the support
she could get.

It was a tour de force of acting.

For the remainder of the weekend, Brett never
found herself alone again with David. She regretted
the faint constraint this caused, but she realised it
had to be. Jay had lost no time admonishing her.

'That's where it ends, Marisa,' he told her.
'Dave's a damned fool allowing himself a romantic
daydream. We wouldn't want it to go sour, would
we?'

'Showing the *real* you?' Brett found herself
taunting him. She had intended to tell him about
Kerri's piece of mischief, but Jay could be
shockingly arrogant when he chose. Let it seem she
had been attracted to David. It sweetened her
mood. Jay's high-handedness went beyond his
rights. She shuddered to think what he would be
like after marriage.

Less than half an hour after their brief clash he
had announced to the whole party their wedding
date: December the twentieth. He held her to him;
he had to. Brett's leg muscles abruptly gave out.

Brett went down to the airstrip to see them all off.
Although she had lived with the idea of her
approaching marriage these past months, she
couldn't believe Jay had set the actual date. Hadn't
he ever heard of asking the bride? Not that she was
a bride—more a business partner. Even business
partners had to be consulted.

David shook her hand, a kind of driven urgency

beneath the courteous, pleasant sentences. 'If you ever need someone to come to ... someone to help you, or just listen, please think of me,' he murmured quickly as Jay turned away to check under the Beech Baron.

Was that David's way of saying he thought she was being used?

Kerri smiled at her with curving lips and blank eyes. 'If I can't be a bridesmaid, at least throw the bouquet at me!'

She had to get to the altar first. All these people, and probably not one of them believed Jay loved her.

'A kiss before I go,' Jay called to her, and Brett could see the mockery blazing out of his eyes.

She moved gracefully towards him, a small, slender girl in an amethyst silk top and matching pants, a double belt resting on her narrow hips. She expected the usual display of allegiance, but some devil had got into Jay. He lifted her clear off the ground so their mouths were on a level, then he kissed her with a sensuality no one was likely to forget.

Brett was reduced to a breathless mumbling. 'You brute!'

His brilliant eyes sparkled, shockingly brilliant eyes. 'If there's anyone winning prizes around here, honey, it's me!'

'What in the world are you talking about?'

'I'm beginning to think Dave's a real old rogue. What was he whispering to you so heroically?'

'His phone number,' hissed Brett.

'I wouldn't be at all surprised.' Jay lowered her gently to the ground. 'See you, little one, take care. I couldn't operate if I didn't know you were safe here.'

Brett groaned. Jay was such an unnerving mixture!

'You might decide to start on our bedroom,' he added with a cool smile. 'Spare no expense. It's going to be our private sanctuary.'

He was about to go, and Brett caught his arm and lifted herself on tiptoe. 'Break just one of the rules and our deal's off,' she whispered in his ear.

'Darling!' He kissed her once again. Hard.

They were all staring out of the plane. Kerri's head was in view. Brett waved and moved away to the Land Rover.

A few minutes later the twin engines roared into life. The aircraft moved down the runway gathering speed for the take-off. It lifted and soared into a cobalt sky. Soon it was a mere speck. Only then did Brett turn away. Her life wasn't hers any more. Perhaps it had never been hers. She couldn't remember a time when it hadn't been Jay's.

The photographs kept up as Brett knew they would. It was a standard underhand practice. She considered sending them on to Jay, but she had already had his response. The fireplace seemed a good choice, but she was still at the stage when she was questioning the morality of her own decisions. Marriage with Jay presented terrible dilemmas— for *her*. Men seemed to have little trouble differentiating between wives and lovers. On the basis of these photographs, recent because Kerri had taken the trouble to have her hair restyled in a distinctive short cut, Jay was her constant companion at

functions. Either that or she had managed to have
herself photographed right beside him. Brett supposed that mightn't be all that difficult for someone
like Kerri Whitman; she had always received a
good deal of society coverage. Jay, of course,
expected her to defer to his male superiority.
Diamond Valley had never been the place to fight
women's rights. Man was king. Jay, for all his
strong protective streak, wasn't all that different
from the knights of the Middle Ages. He expected
to be obeyed without question. He expected to be
trusted implicitly no matter how devastating his
actions purported to be.

Brett had seen him with Kerri. For that matter,
over the years she had seen him with a lot of
beautiful girls. There was once a girl called Sally he
had liked very much. Brett had liked her too.
Whenever she came to Diamond Valley, which was
often, she had always brought the much younger
Brett a nice surprise. Sally had been exceptional.
Kerri Whitman and her friends had treated her as
an oddity in the Carradine set-up. People like Kerri
and Elaine had seen that the stories abounded.

In the end, Brett didn't destroy the photographs
at all; she kept them as she had the ones Jay had so
carelessly thrown away. If nothing else they
established beyond question that both parties were
extremely photogenic. Brett decided at going on
twenty-one—of course December the twentieth was
her birthday—it was about time she stopped
allowing people to manipulate her. It was all very
well for Jay to tuck her neatly out of sight while he
lived a full, dynamic life, but she had to follow her
own path to true adult identity. Much as she loved

Jay—and the thought of losing him drove her to despair—nothing really good could come of a marriage without love. She knew arranged marriages happened and many appeared to work very well, but such a marriage was potentially traumatic for her. Behind her hard-won reserve she was a deeply sensitive and emotional woman. Jay, if no one else, had the power to destroy her. She had given him her promise and she had a conscience about promises, but now she required guarantees.

The following week when Carradine Air Freight flew into the property with all sorts of things she had ordered Brett took advantage of a free trip down to Adelaide, the beautiful capital of South Australia. She advised no one of her visit, including Jay. With shoulder-length, naturally deep-waving hair she didn't need a hairdresser all that frequently. Often she simply trimmed her hair herself or had one of the housegirls help her amid waves of giggles. Now she decided on a style. She had seen it in a magazine. The model was her type, large-eyed, small-boned, with a curling cloud of hair. The model's hair had been graduated in length to release the natural curl and Brett thought the same style would suit her very well.

She intended to buy lots of clothes as well. The woman in Jay's life would have to realise she had a lifetime of fierce competition ahead of her. Jay radiated a vivid sexuality, and such a quality had attendant dangers. Brett was stuck with the same quality herself and failed to recognise it. She had never *used* her beauty at any time. Her mother had been a very beautiful woman and she had suffered for it. Brett identified beauty and suffering in her own mind.

To other women, like Kerri Whitman, beauty was a symbol of power. Kerri's good looks had given her endless gratification. It had begun with, 'What a beautiful baby!' and it had never stopped. Brett, for a variety of reasons, not the least of them growing up in a male-dominated environment, unconnected with family, had an altogether different conception of her femininity.

She had never been the centre of anyone's universe. With her advanced intelligence she had realised even at an early age that her mother had placed a *man* before her child. That man had been J.B. Her inheritance was his way of making reparation. She would gladly have swopped it for the kind of childhood and adolescence many of her student friends had enjoyed.

Was it possible that in marrying Jay she would only be perpetuating her mother's life? She realised now she wanted more. Much more.

It was an exquisite figure indeed who emerged from Celine's Boutique. As a student and at home on Diamond Valley Brett had never had much more than a small collection of clothes. In the past hours she had had her hair styled, bought an entire range of Estee Lauder beauty products, several of the French perfumes that most appealed to her, and a high fashion wardrobe for every conceivable occasion. Accessories were included too. So unfamiliar was she with such lavish self-indulgence, she thought she must surely have outfitted herself for life. She didn't realise then how much appearance counted in Jay's world. The women in rich men's lives were expected to look superb. It was taken for granted. Even a woman whose preoccupation wasn't clothes was made to realise her appearance reflected on her husband. If she was to be seen at Jay's side, a role Kerri Whitman appeared to be usurping, she would have to look very fashionable indeed.

Celine and others had only been too happy to oblige. Celine, a Frenchwoman, who travelled back and forth from Australia to Europe, was renowned for her magnificent range of clothes, and the artist in her responded keenly to hanging favourite garments on such a beautiful clothes horse. Although petite, Brett was perfectly proportioned, with the model-girl requirements of long neck, small breasts, narrow waist and hips and long graceful limbs.

By the time Celine had finished with her, Brett felt ready for anything, even the functions Kerri Whitman and her circle were likely to attend. She was a rich girl now—not '*that* woman's daughter'. There was no need to wait for Jay to give her jewellery either; she could buy it herself. She had lived all her life under a system of male domination. As much as J.B. had favoured her, he had never set her free.

Brett had always loved pearls, so now she bought a long lustrous string and matching earrings. She was wearing a stylish silk two-piece in white patterned with swirls of blue, rose and lavender. The pearls were the perfect complement, glowing softly against her beautiful skin. No one hurried away to check on her credit. Whatever her past, she was a woman of consequence now. How money did talk! These days it positively opened doors, but tragedy and unhappiness were intrinsic to the human species. Brett had begun life with nothing, but from what she had seen she had been no worse off in terms of conflicts than the very rich.

Still, it was wonderful to be financially independent, even if in the middle of it she had to pinch herself to make sure she wasn't dreaming. No man was her master. Or so she told herself.

CHAPTER SIX

THE head offices of the Carradine Corporation occupied several of the top floors in the city's most prestigious executive building. Brett had never been inside until this very year; J.B. had not wanted her there. Now his death gave her instant access.

'Good afternoon, Miss Sargent,' a smart young woman said to her immediately she stepped out of the lift. The young woman was carrying a number of files she had been instructed to take down to the legal office.

Brett smiled pleasantly and walked to the reception desk. All the offices were spacious, spotless, quietly opulent. They presented the traditional look, symbolic of the Carradine way of living, rather than the bold and blunt modern format. The staff were very well trained and a smart appearance was considered a prerequisite rather than a valuable asset.

The receptionist, a beautifully groomed blonde impeccably attired, gave Brett a dazzling smile and reached for the phone. 'I'll tell Mr Carradine you're here.'

'Please—I'm looking to surprise him.'

The blonde blinked her long eyelashes. Brett interpreted that as meaning she wasn't sure that was at all wise.

It was really like a giant beehive. Every little section had its own leader, but instead of a queen bee, there was Jay. He occupied the throne room, so lately the province of his father. It was Jay who made all the important final decisions, but in general his top executives were left in charge of their own domains. Brett had put a great deal of time and concentration into studying the various phases of the business, but its scope was increasing all the time. As soon as she had learned that Morton and Elaine wanted to sell Diamond Valley off Brett had begun thinking of ways to make the homestead pay. There was no question that it cost a fortune to maintain, and there was a problem for either of the brothers to find the time to even get there. Morton considered that the many millions such a pastoral jewel would bring could be put to better use: expanding Carradine Aviation, for example. They could buy more helicopters, aeroplanes. They now operated one of the largest fleet of jets in Australia with a twenty-four-hour, seven-day-a-week service. It had occurred to Brett that the homestead would make a very grand private hotel for the swarms of overseas visitors, particularly from Japan and America who had heard of the powerful scenery the Australian Outback offered and wished to explore it. With Carradine Aviation already operating in the area charter flights could be made to all the vast desert monuments, which were truly wonderful, as well as the splendours of Katherine Gorge and that paradise of the wild, Arnhem Land. Brett had had long enough to gauge the reaction of overseas visitors to the station. They revelled in the splendid comfort of the homestead. They were amazed at the starkly sublime beauty of the Centre and the incredible lushness of the North.

It was a thought, and so far she had kept it to herself.

Jay's secretary ran her territory like a general. Unlike the receptionists she was neither young nor beautiful. She was a rather severe-looking woman in her late forties and she enjoyed executive status.

'Ah, good afternoon, Miss Sargent.' A discreet but extremely thorough head-to-toe examination. 'How well you look! This *is* a surprise.'

'Mr Carradine in?' Brett returned the practised smile.

'Why, yes.' The secretary gave her another packed look. 'He's extremely busy, but I'll tell him you're here.'

'Please—don't bother.'Brett realised she *had* altered. She would never have spoken like that once. Surely it had a dash of Jay's cool arrogance?

Jay was sitting behind his desk, head down. He looked intensely handsome, intensely formidable in his dark business clothes.

'Leave it there, thank you, Avril, and get my brother on the phone.'

'Is it too far to walk down the corridor?' asked Brett.

His head flew up in startled recognition. His blue eyes seared her to the spot.

'If looks could kill!'

'As in devour?' He stood up. 'I was wondering how long it would take you to fly the coop. I figured on just about now. You look exquisite.'

'I do?' She gave him a little cool smile that actually concealed a tremendous, chronic longing.

'Exquisite is an understatement.' He held her shoulders and allowed his gaze to roam all over her.

'I think you've been here before. You know too
much to have learned it in one lifetime. I didn't
think it possible to paint a lily, but the effect is
dazzling. Where did you get those pearls? I don't
recall having seen them.'

'I bought them with my own money.'

'It used to be a husband's privilege to buy his
wife's jewellery,' he pointed out drily.

'I couldn't wait,' shrugged Brett.

'No one ever said you *had* to wait. Tell me where
you bought them.'

'Oh, a jeweller. A very good one.' She threw back
her shining head. With the full weight of her hair
layered it framed her face in a dark cloud of waves
and curls. It was normally parted on the side, but
the stylist had changed it to the centre, accentuating
the perfect symmetry of her features. In one stroke
he had created the ideal look for her. Her beauty
was essentially classical, and the manner in which
she now wore her hair embellished that look.

Jay seemed amused by her insouciance. 'Am I
allowed to kiss that glossy mouth?'

'Since when did you *ask*?' she said drily.

'Since when did you start looking like a million-
airess? You aren't little Brett any longer. I guess
you've passed your final test.' He bent his dark
head, his mouth just touching hers.

It was extraordinary. She wanted to move away,
knowing he was tormenting her, for whatever
reason, but her yearning was too much. Her sweet
breath came into his mouth as a fevered little sigh
and abruptly, masterfully, he folded her into his
arms.

They stayed like that together, mouths locked.

There was a starburst behind Brett's eyes. Her body agonised to be closer to his. He was kissing her so deeply she could hardly stand.

'*Jay!*' She might have cried to him, '*Help me!*'

'I want you so much I can't take this any more.' His fingers circled her breast, then he pushed back abruptly.

'Where are you staying?' he asked.

She named the hotel, breathing deeply to overcome her raging blood.

'Does Gran know you're here?'

'No one. I thought it was about time I did my own thing.'

'I want you to go to her.'

'She may not want me.'

'You can't believe that,' he challenged her, almost curtly. 'I don't want you in some hotel by yourself. There's no need. I'll put through a call to Gran now.'

A moment later he was speaking to his grandmother, then he passed Brett the phone. The warmth and pleasure in Mrs Chase's voice brought comfort into Brett's guarded heart. Making the transition to *family* would be easy with such a generous, gracious lady, but Brett knew she might never be accepted by other members of a tightly knit clan.

'I'll arrange for your things to be sent over from the hotel.' Jay turned back to his desk with his quick, lithe tread. 'I wouldn't bother mentioning to Gran that you checked into a hotel. She'd be hurt.'

'I think she might understand,' Brett murmured, low-voiced. 'I'm bound to see Morton and Elaine.'

'I expect so, if you pass the lodge every day.

Morton's all right, Brett. His feelings are mixed about you. He always wanted to like you, but he couldn't. The way J.B. brought us all up was enough to tie anyone in knots. For a long time Morton couldn't deal with J.B.'s rejection. All those rages and the cruel teasing were a result of jealousy, a terrible state of rivalry J.B. created. Now that he's gone, we can all settle down. In a very short time you're going to be my wife.'

'Aren't you going to add "when we straighten out the details"?' queried Brett.

'*What* details?' he asked softly, a brittle smile on his mouth.

'We don't love one another, Jay, I know that, but I would need your promise to be faithful. I'd never allow you to touch me if you weren't.'

'Do you want to bet?' His voice dropped dangerously, an insolent smile in his eyes.

'It won't come to that.' She bit her full bottom lip. 'Marriage without fidelity would lose all its value.'

'There's a genuine mystery here,' Jay said shortly. 'Who the hell am I going to be unfaithful with? Is it Kerri? *Again*?'

'Well, more photographs did arrive.'

'Which *you* think have some significance?'

'Don't go all glittery with me, Jay. I learned to cope years ago. What I'm really saying is, whatever your relationship with Kerri Whitman in the past, it would have to stop.'

'You offensive little brat!' he growled.

'Not at all—I'm just your fiancée. If I ever get your ring on my finger, that is.'

'So where is it now?'

'I pawned it around noon.' Brett couldn't hold the

sharpness in. He took a few steps towards her and
she made a convulsive little movement of retreat.
'It's in my bag.'

'What happened? Couldn't you bear it between
your breasts?'

'Jay, the gold chain wouldn't go with the pearls.'

He put out his right hand and lifted the lustrous
strand.

'Surely you're not going to rip them off?'

'I'm funny about a lot of things.'

'Jay!' she protested.

His brilliant glance slanted unpleasantly over
her. 'You think you know me, little one? You're
only just learning. *I know we don't love one another,'*
he brutally mimicked her words. 'What *is* love, do
you know? All those feelings you can't control. *I*
can't control. I'd have to suggest to you that it's the
longest lasting lust on record. Maybe it even
happens every hundred years. Get *my* ring out of
your bag.'

Colour burned along her high, delicate cheekbones. 'Do you expect me to obey that tone of
voice?'

'I certainly do. You're a beautiful, articulate,
intelligent girl, Marisa, but I'm much stronger than
you are. I'll just take hold of you——'

'I'll get it. I'll get it to avoid an unpleasant scene.'
She walked to his huge mahogany desk and picked
up her soft leather handbag. 'I suppose if I'd been
somone else you'd have given me a party.'

His eyes narrowed to slits and the lean line of his
jaw tightened.' What is it you're looking for, to go
over my knee? We held off as a mark of respect to
J.B., or have you conveniently forgotten?'

'I'm sorry.'She felt herself go a little white. Jay when he was angry was all glittery male energy. She took the ring out of her bag but couldn't hold it, her hands were trembling so much. It slipped through her fingers and rolled on the carpet.

'We'll have dinner tonight,' he said curtly. 'Just you and me. You can have the biggest party you like a week before the wedding.' He bent and picked up the ring. 'You're *not* going to get out of it. Clearly you're getting cold feet. I promise to stay stone cold sober. I promise not to touch you unless you want it. I will *not* promise to be faithful. I consider it a serious slur on my character. Someone starts a rumour and it spreads. You'll hear plenty of rumours when you're married to me. You're a major problem in yourself. I can see you haven't got a clue what I'm saying,' he added. 'Don't you ever look in the mirror? What do you think you're seeing, little Snow White? You're an enchantress, Brett. Men are going to fall for you in droves.'

'If you want to break my fingers, you're doing a good job,' she cried emotionally.

'I want to wrap your hair around your throat and strangle you, if you want to know.' His blue eyes were flashing warning signals.

'You're horrible, horrible! You push the ring on my finger.'

'For God's sake, stop it!' He pulled her into his arms, dragging her head back. 'Stop it, do you hear?'

She shut her eyes as though she couldn't bear to look at him, and his mouth came down and covered hers.

Anger raised their passion to a new key. Brett

thought she was surely fainting. Her graceful body seemed to go slack against his, but he wouldn't release her so easily. He kissed her into a half dazed submission, then with appalling suddenness lifted his head.

'You deserved that. You know you did.' Sexual hostility glittered in his brilliant eyes.

Brett's whole body was trembling from the force of his passion. She could barely open her eyes, her small panting breaths betraying her extreme agitation. 'I'm sorry I came here,' she whispered.

'You ought to be sorry for a lot!' grated Joy,

'*Tell* me,' she gasped. 'For the past twenty years? For my *mother*? For J.B. because he cared for me? Probably you're only thinking of marrying me to get your hands on the money!'

'It certainly couldn't be love,' he laughed harshly, his face darkly relentless.

She wanted to hit him. She *hated* him. She hated him so much she was barely able to keep from sobbing her heart out.

Jay muffled an oath and grasped her creamy nape. 'I have a feeling, Brett, that we're getting angry for the same reason. I don't know what it looks like to you, but you're in my blood. You know my history, I know yours. We're hopelessly entwined.'

Memories took wing and her face crumpled in pain.

'Don't you cry,' he said softly. 'Don't you *dare* cry.'

She let her head fall forward against his shoulder and abruptly his hand lost its tension and fell to caressing the long line of her neck. Jay's other arm caught her into him, the fire transmuted to an odd tenderness.

'Do you really think I want your money?' he asked sardonically.

Brett shook her head.

'I can't hear you, Marisa.'

'No, Jay.'

'I think I'm doing a pretty fair job of increasing your fortune.'

'I had so much to tell you,' she sighed.

He lifted her head and tilted up her chin. Her eyes were enormous, shimmering with tears. 'It breaks my heart just to look at you,' he said quietly.

'Is something wrong with my face?' She blinked her lashes quickly, thinking her delicate make-up might be ruined.

'God, what a question!' His mouth twisted wryly. 'You've lost all your lipstick, but I don't think it matters—men kiss their fiancées all the time. The ring is on. Keep it on. We've waited long enough.'

The Board called an important, unscheduled meeting for the following week. Brett attended, but her part was restricted to listening to what Jay and various members said. Inside information had been leaked to a senior Carradine executive that a rival air-freight company, generally believed to be thriving, was having significant internal problems and was ripe for a take-over. The current Managing Director, known to everyone at the table, outside Brett, was said to be failing to maximise profit, a cardinal sin. As well, management were having increasing problems with their personnel. The company, the Board was told, was riddled with

conflicts and though it was highly unlikely it would
collapse in the short term, in the long term it was
risking bankruptcy. The time for Carradine to act
was now. Westgate could not rival Carradine, but
the Board agreed that a take-over would greatly
increase Carradine power. One thing was important, however: until Carradine made its raid there
was to be absolute secrecy as to the Board's
intentions. A leak to the business world, to the
press, would be fatal. Industrial spying was a
constant threat to modern business. The Carradine
informant was a key man in the Westgate hierar-
chy. As a trade, he expected to be given a similar
position within the Carradine Corporation.

It seemed to Brett he wasn't much of a man to be
trusted, but it seemed he had worked long and hard
for his own organisation, but when he couldn't
change the present decision-making, he justified his
actions by saying he was ultimately concerned with
the survival of a business he had helped build up.

It was on this issue the Board argued. Finally it
was agreed that the Westgate executive had been
motivated solely by his anger and impotence at
seeing in his own words, 'a good company go fast
down the drain'. As a rationale it was generally
understood. No money was involved. The aim was
to save Westgate. A take-over by Carradine
represented in terms of profit, efficiency and
control the best option available.

Voting was unanimous.

Brett was returning to Jay's office when she saw
Elaine walking down the corridor. Elaine, with her
attenuated figure, was looking very high fashion in
a torso-hugging jacket and narrow skirt in elegant

black and white. She wore a hat with a little spotted veil, and whatever their marked differences Brett decided she had never known a time when Elaine didn't look stunning.

Elaine, for her part, had decided she had better not ignore Brett's presence any more. She flashed the younger girl a bright, false smile.

'Meeting broken up, has it?'

'Just this minute. You look terrific, Elaine, as usual.'

'It's absolutely no use looking anything else,' Elaine agreed carelessly. 'Someone has obviously taken *you* in hand,' she added.

'I didn't have a great deal of money in the old days.'

'Well, you have now, dear,' Elaine drawled acidly. 'I see you're wearing your ring.'

'Jay wants me to.'

'Ummm——' Elaine couldn't seem to tear her eyes away from the magnificence of the ring, the huge central sapphire set with baguette diamonds. 'How does it feel to have snared one of the biggest matrimonial prizes in the country? A guy, incidentally, who belonged to somebody else?'

Brett threw up her head sharply, her luminous eyes trained on Elaine's face. 'It's good to be loyal to one's friends, but on the subject of Kerri Whitman you really ought to sort out the facts,' she said calmly. 'Kerri had high hopes, I know. I'm sorry if she's suffering, but even without me I doubt very much whether Jay would have gone on and married her.'

'He *told* her he would,' Elaine laughed cynically. 'I think he would have, dear, but for the nightmare of J.B.'s will. Whether you marry Jay or not, I would *worry* about Kerri, if I were you. I'm quite sure she'll be around to add to your troubles. Of course your particular case mightn't find its way into the divorce courts, but sophisticated people know how to arrange their affairs.'

'Then you ought to go shopping for a new photographer!'

It was a shot in the dark, but the effect on Elaine was spectacular. Her face went slack with shock, then as Brett continued to stare at her challengingly she adopted a façade of aggression.

'What the devil is *that* supposed to mean?'

'Shouldn't you have said, "Photographer?" and looked blank? You didn't look blank, Elaine. You looked stunned. I might have known. Who else could it be? You and Kerri are such pals.'

'You know, I'm sorry for you,' Elaine gasped. 'You're raving! I know nothing whatever about photographs.'

'Even if they've got your fingerprints all over them?'

'I don't see how   ' Elaine broke off abruptly.

'Did you use gloves, you and Kerri? If you thought *I* was going to be upset, you must be crazy. Jay put this ring on my finger because he wants to marry me. If I were you and Kerri I wouldn't worry about why he wants to marry me. *Why* he wants me to be the mother of his son. Speculation will get neither of you anywhere.'

'I've come here to have lunch with Morton,' Elaine complained bitterly. 'I shall tell him what you've said.'

'I bet you won't.' Brett went on taking stabs in the

dark. 'He's coming out of the board room door now. He's smiling at Jay. It's obvious enough he loves his brother, no matter how hard you've tried to change that. Tell him in front of me if you like.Tell him what I've accused you and Kerri Whitman of and I'll stick around to study his face. I think Morton understands you very well. You're the sort of woman who enjoys starting little fires. Here he comes now . . .'

Underneath her chic veil, Elaine's face went pale. 'I always said you're an awful little bitch,' she mumbled. 'Out to get everything you can.'

'Smile, Elaine,' Brett returned coolly. 'We're all going to be one happy family.'

Morton's tall, heavy figure loomed up before them.

'What do you say if we all go out together for lunch?' He looked from one woman to the other. It was clear he was in a good mood.

'Why, that would be lovely, darling,' cooed Elaine, 'but Brett's just told me she has an appointment.'

'Can't you break it?' Morton didn't want his mood ruined.

'It's really something I can't get out of, Morton,' Brett murmured in a disappointed tone. 'Perhaps we could all get together for dinner one evening?' Some time in the far distant future.

'We haven't taken Gran out lately,' Morton seemed infused with good spirits. 'I think we should. They tell me that new place, Colonnades, is very good. Old Berkeley's in town. We should make up a party.'

'That will be great!' Elaine's fair, faintly feral

face convulsed with agonised pleasure. She moved forward a few steps and clasped her husband's arm. 'We should go, darling, if we want them to hold our table.'

Morton laughed again. 'And when have they ever failed to do that? See you later, Brett.' His blue eyes took on their familiar hot glow. 'As someone said in the boardroom just now, you look a dream.'

Something was missing from the dream.

At six o'clock that evening Brett received a phone call from Jay's office requesting her to meet him there as he was unable to get to the house to pick her up. They had made plans to go to the theatre, a new play, and afterwards to go on to supper, but a late appointment had delayed him. Brett did not question it; both brothers worked late many nights.

She thought her quick dressing was a shade too sketchy. She would have liked a little more time, but when she showed herself off to Mrs Chase, that gracious lady smiled with pleasure.

'Beautiful, Brett   just beautiful! I'm so glad lace has come back into fashion. That black goes superbly with white skin.'

Brett didn't hesitate. She bent down and kissed Mrs Chase's fine, dry cheek. 'You're a good girl, Brett,' the old lady patted her hand soothingly. 'You always were and you always will be. I'm happy about this marriage. You have so many fine qualities Jay can only love and respect you.'

All the way into the city, and the Chase chauffeur drove her in, Brett considered how she could secure these twin prizes, love and respect. Jay was a hunter, yet protecting his womenfolk was one of his

most powerful instincts. It was easy to recall the
many times Jay had put himself at risk saving her
from possible injury. As a child on the station she
had tried desperately to be self-reliant. Her mother
had not been able to spare her a great deal of time,
and because Brett so terribly needed her mother she
had been driven to an exaggerated independence.
Moving so freely about a great station had often put
her in physical danger. Jay had always been there.
To a great extent, and she saw that now, he had
played a near-parental role. Jay had watched over
her through every stage. It *had* to be caring. Or had
it been pity for a little girl largely deprived of a
normal childhood? One thing was understood: their
lives, as he had said, were hopelessly entwined.
Surely that was central to an enduring relationship.
Perhaps, as she so desperately wanted to, she should
tell him what he meant to her, what he had meant to
her over all these long years. It shouldn't be
difficult, yet the circumstances of her life had made
her fear showing her heart. Self-denial was long
instilled. She was overly cautious about everything.

There was a hush over the top floor. Everyone
had gone home. Brett walked quietly down the
corridor and into Jay's suite. His door was ajar, but
as she went to go forward to give it a little rap she
was startled by the sound of low, angry voices.

She fell back against Jay's secretary's desk. She
needed to. The voices she had heard belonged to Jay
and a woman he apparently couldn't get out of his
life: Kerri Whitman. She waited a minute and the
voices stopped. Perhaps she had made a little
involuntary sound. She wanted to run away, but she
knew she had to face it. Incidents like these broke

engagements. What she had been attempting to do was live a lie. She had more pride than that.

Brett drew herself up and reached for the doorknob, throwing the heavy door wide open.

What she saw seared itself into her brain. Kerri Whitman, in a dishevelled state, was trapped in Jay's arms. Another thing came to her: Jay had just lifted his head from kissing her. His face was darkened with passion and Brett felt all her flimsy hopes fly out the window. 'I think I've got the message now,' she said quietly. 'It's obvious you two can't keep apart.'

She didn't want to scream, to rave and rant: she just wanted to disappear in a puff of smoke. Like her dreams. She was pulling off the great sapphire ring, but neither was it her way to throw it. She put it down gently on one of the bookshelves that lined the wall.

'I think you might ask what the hell is going on?' Jay exploded violently, giving the incredible impression that he and not she was the one deeply wronged. He almost threw Kerri from him and she burst into near hysterical laughter.

'I warned you, didn't I, you stupid girl? You never quite got it before.'

Brett didn't need a warning now. She turned and fled down the corridor.

Jay came after her, but the lift was waiting and she closed the door in his face. Trust Jay to look like an avenging archangel! He was showing his true nature. The rules of man didn't apply to him.

He almost caught her as she hurried across the foyer. What on earth did he think he was going to say? He ought to be able to have his cake and eat it too? Men were incredible creatures. Hadn't J.B. treated her mother the same way?

There was a taxi stand on the other side of the street, and so anxious was Brett to get to it she looked swiftly both ways but not back again. A small blue sedan raced around the corner on the lights, coming directly for her, and as the taxi driver shouted in horror, he saw a man swoop from the pavement and lift the girl backwards and almost clear off the ground. The man threw himself back, but as he pivoted the sedan struck him glancingly before stopping amid a squeal of brakes.

The two of them fell to the ground.

The taxi driver waited no more. He leapt out of his car and raced to their assistance. The driver of the blue sedan, swearing profusely, pulled over into a NO STANDING zone.

'Boy, that was close!' The tall, lean man needed no assistance, but the taxi driver helped him lift the girl to her feet. 'I thought you were a goner, young lady,' he insisted. 'Probably the bloke in the car was going too fast.'

'I'm sorry . . . so sorry.' Brett was terribly shaken.

'*Sorry?*' The single word seemed to flame from Jay and the taxi driver raised his eyebrows.

'I think you should check nothing's broken. You okay, mister?'

'Nothing much wrong with me,' the tall man said briskly. 'Thanks for coming to our assistance.'

'Sure was a near thing. When you feel up to it, little lady, you ought to thank this nice gentleman. I reckon you'd be lying in an ambulance by now. Just look what you've done to your stockings—and oh, your *elbow*!'

'I'll take care of her,' said the tall man.

The taxi-driver decided they knew one another after all. Couldn't be lovers; their behaviour was too odd. The girl had come out of that office building. Come to think of it, he knew the guy—Carradine, that was it. Not only was he rich, he was brave.

The driver of the blue sedan needed calming and reassuring, and Brett, to prevent further interest, as a small crowd had quickly gathered, went with Jay back inside the building.

'Let's have a look,' he clipped when they were inside the lift.

'I can attend to it, Jay. It's nothing.' In fact she had badly grazed her elbow.

'You might have been killed!'

'I wasn't. You always seem to be close by.'

'Just an old habit.' He was white beneath his dark bronze tan. 'If you're wondering, I'm quite sure Kerri Whitman has gone.'

'I guess she got a kick out of seeing me nearly go under a car,' shrugged Brett. 'If she came out the front door she couldn't have missed it.'

'I'd say she went down to the parking lot.'

'The car hit you. Are you hurt?'

'Don't sound so hopeful!' he said bitterly.

'I would never want you hurt, Jay. You've been good enough to me in your fashion, after all.'

The lift stopped at the top floor and he guided her along the corridor. 'I was just about to come for you. What the devil were you doing here?'

'Ask your secretary.' Brett felt so shaken she was sick.

'You bet I will! Avril had no instructions from me to ring you.'

'Maybe not Avril. I understood it was someone from your office.'

'Man or woman?' Jay stopped and looked down at her frowningly.

'A woman. Aren't they all?' Brett slowly lifted her head. What she was going to say failed. There was such a look of anger and concern in Jay's eyes, her bitterness left her.

'Hold me,' she whispered. The very ground seemed to tremble beneath her.

Immediately his arms came around her. 'Stay here,' he murmured. 'Stay here where you belong.'

His jacket coat brushed against her tender skin and she gave a little shiver of pain.

'We'd better clean that up, I guess.'

'I've scarcely felt it.'

'You've skinned it raw. I think I'll get Kendall to take a look at it.'

'It's nothing, Jay.' She twisted her arm so she could take a closer look at her elbow. 'I've had worse falls.'

'You've never jumped in front of a cab before.'

Jay sat her down in his office while he went for the first-aid kit. Brett was feeling so shaky she left all her thoughts alone. Time for that later. She relived the moment when Jay had hauled her away from that car. She knew that he had risked injury. That dimension of their troubled relationship had not left them; when she was in trouble he went to her aid.

'I know *you* must be badly bruised,' she pointed out wretchedly when he had joined her.

'My dear Marisa, I'm tough,' he assured her.

'I suppose you are.'

'This might hurt a bit,' he warned.

Brett drew in her breath He swabbed the whole area, gently patted it dry, then brushed it with an antibiotic powder. 'I'll just put some gauze around it, then I'll take you back to my apartment. We can have something to eat there.'

'I want to go home, Jay,' she said quietly.

'Isn't *home* with me?'

'The house we're trying to build has too many cracks in it. They seem to get wider every day.'

'Ever heard of sabotage?' He finished tying a neat dressing.

She put a trembling hand over her face. 'Not now, Jay. I feel a little sick.'

'Then you'll come with me. For better or worse, Marisa, I'm the man in your life.'

For the rest of the evening he was kind and solicitous. While Brett tidied herself up and removed her ruined stockings he went to the phone and ordered dinner for two from a restaurant he frequented. It was not the restaurant's usual practice to cater for the home, but anything for Mr Carradine.

While they waited Brett rested quietly on the richly-hued glove leather banquette. Jay's apartment was bold and masculine—powerful, like his personality. The walls were all dark, gleaming timber. The tufted leather on the banquettes around the room matched the upholstery on the antique dining chairs. The table was very modern with a top of some sparkling stone. The art works too were very modern and compelling, for Jay was a man with strong and wide-ranging aesthetic tastes and opinions. Diamond Valley was traditional; this was avant-garde.

Forty minutes later, the food arrived—avocado with seafood, lobster Newburg and a fragrant, delicious iced dessert made with tropical fruits.

Jay seated her at the table and poured the wine. It simply wasn't real. The two of them ignored the events of the past hours; Jay knew instinctively it wasn't the time to face them. Brett shut them out. Jay had an immediate and extortionate effect on her emotions. She loved him so much that though she might bleed inside she was ready to forgive him. This fact alone proved conclusively that women were more forgiving than men.

He took her home towards midnight when they were sure Mrs Chase would have gone to bed. Both of them recognised an unwritten rule that the boys' grandmother should not be disturbed or upset. Lillian Chase had suffered a number of tragedies in her life; she was entitled to a little peace at nearing eighty.

The Lodge was still ablaze as they swept past. Morton and Elaine entertained frequently, for big parties at the Main House when Mrs Chase gave her permission, but for small affairs at the splendidly renovated and refurbished Lodge. Brett glanced briefly at the driveway beneath the canopy of great shade trees and immediately felt sick to the pit of her stomach. Kerri Whitman's white Porsche stood out against the dark purple shadows.

Jay with his characteristic alertness noticed it as soon as they drove through the great wrought iron gates.

'Would you be completely rocked if we tackled this thing now?' He pulled the Jaguar over and turned to face her.

'Surely you don't want to go in now?'

His blue eyes glittered. '*I'm* going, Marisa, even if you're not. No woman makes a fool out of me!'

She could feel her whole being recoil. 'None of them are on my side, Jay. Kerri is Elaine's friend. Nothing would please Elaine more than to see our engagement break up. Morton is of the same mind.'

'I don't think you understand exactly how Morton feels. Morton is a little mixed up about you, certainly, but I can assure you he'd much rather see me with you than anyone like Kerri Whitman. Kerri is Elaine's friend, not Morton's. Morton is my *brother*. Do you know what that means? The blood bond is *real*. Kerri is a good-looking woman with lots of sex appeal, but she thinks nothing of cheap acts. I know why. Morton knows too. I just have to prove it to you.'

'All right, Jay,' Brett barely whispered.

Morton came to the door, his welcoming smile stopping short when he saw his brother's face and Brett's bandaged arm. 'Hey, what's gone wrong?' He held back the door and ushered them in. 'Elaine,' he called over his shoulder, 'Jay and Brett are here. This must be the night for upset— Kerri arrived a couple of hours ago. Elaine's been feeding her Scotch and sympathy.'

'Jay!' Elaine rushed out into the hallway, her voice more high-pitched than normal. She looked down dismayed at Brett's arm. 'Come in. Come in!'

'You've got Kerri out the back,' Jay broke in brutally. 'Trot her out.'

'What the heck's going on?' Morton rumpled his blond head.

'Let's make it short and sweet,' responded Jay, his handsome face with the strength and glitter of polished steel. 'Kerri is trying to wreck our engagement and she's getting some help.'

'What the hell!' Morton groaned.

'You know what else, old spunk?'Jay advanced on his brother. 'Your sweet wife is up to her ears in suspicion.'

Morton waved to the sofas in the living room. 'Can't we all sit down? I mean, I'm a stranger in my own home. I never know what's going on.'

Elaine looked white and a little bit tipsy. 'I don't know what you mean, Jay. Kerri came here tonight to talk to me.'

'Are you going to get her or shall I fetch her out?' Jay's white teeth snapped together.

Kerri herself appeared at the open doorway. 'Don't bother, I'm here. Is this going to be a *wonderful* get-together!'

'More like a confession!' Jay threw up his dark head, anger and arrogance in his expression. 'You're starting to wobble, Kerri. Don't you think you'd better sit down?'

'Certainly, if it's going to make you explain.' Kerri advanced into the room and sat down carefully beside her friend. 'Has dear little Brett hurt herself?' Her hazel eyes glinted with thinly veiled contempt.

Jay turned sharply, looking even more dangerous. 'I don't think you're grasping the magnitude of your mistakes. I can only point out that my influence is far-reaching. I don't as a rule make war on women, but then I've never found myself so angry before.'

'Isn't that natural?' drawled Kerri 'Your fiancée has found you out '

'My fiancée has been sent a lot of photographs,' Jay announced curtly 'I advised her to throw them on the fire, as they didn't interest me They've been upsetting her So now I take action '

Elaine gasped and put her hand to her heart Jay's look of stormy vitality was never more in evidence 'Can't you just let it be, Jay? What good would it do?'

'We could make sure who took them. We know why. Further, tonight Brett received a phone call telling her to meet me at my office instead of waiting for me up at the house as arranged. Anyone could see it as a set-up, but she went. Kerri made sure she was there before her. She staged an angry scene and obviously she saw it as a final performance, because she made herself as dishevelled as she could in the shortest possible time. She even shoved her hands through her hair and tore open her blouse— the one she's wearing now. It was intended to stop Brett in her tracks, and it did. She took off her ring and tried to put as much distance between us as she could. She was almost knocked over by a car.'

'Brett was?' Morton jerked his head around sharply.

'Fortunately I caught up with her and managed to pull her away.'

Kerri laughed.

It's no joke!'

Elaine shut her eyes.

'What's the most startling thing here,' Kerri drawled, 'is the wild distortion of Jay's story. I could

scarcely deny that I presented a—what was it?—
dishevelled image, but then I've always been drawn
to a violent lover. It's a case of now he wants me,
now he don't.'

'I won't settle for anything less than the truth,'
Jay said bluntly, ignoring her flippancy.

'Your truth isn't mine, darling.'

'I'll try to remember that when your brother
comes to renew his contract.'

For the first time a chill seemed to ripple through
Kerri's ultra-slim body. 'What has Graham to do
with this?' It was more of an aggrievement than a
question.

Jay gave a twisted smile. 'Who started out with
the cheap weapons?'

'You were my lover, were you not?'

'I usually don't talk, but you don't seem to have
any such inhibitions. We indulged our sexual urges
from time to time. As far as I can recall it was
pleasant, but so long ago it's all blurred.'

'Jay!' It was Brett who spoke. 'Please—no more.'

'Can't take it, dear?' Kerri sneered at her.

'I don't like to see you humiliated.' It was said so
quietly, so sincerely, the effect was shattering.

Kerri, a strong, determined young woman, burst
into wild sobbing and Elaine put her arms around
her protectively.

'Are you satisfied now?'

'Why don't you tell us *your* part in it?' Jay
retaliated. 'All those crocodile tears don't help. I've
learned that a woman thinks she can get away with
murder if she sheds a few tears. Always in *my* mind
is protecting Brett. She's not a sharp-tongued snob,
like you two.'

'Hang on, Jay,' Morton interrupted. 'I can understand you're angry——'

'You don't know *how* angry. Brett could have been killed tonight!'

'It's all terribly unfortunate,'Morton said helplessly. 'What the hell *did* you do, Elaine?'

'Hold on. Did I say I did anything?'

'I've had my answer.' Brett stood up. 'See this on my arm? I did that. I blame no one. I accept that Kerri once knew Jay very well, but *she* must accept that that is now over. I'm prepared to try and forget it all.'

Elaine shook her blonde head stubbornly. 'I have no connection with all this. I'm merely being a good friend.'

'You might have remembered you're attacking family before you started,' Jay told her uncompromisingly. 'I'd like a guarantee from you, Morton, that you'll keep your wife in order. She's getting too far over the mark these days. I wouldn't like to have to drop a word in Gerald's ear. If anyone knows his daughter, he does.'

'Leave it to me, Jay.' Morton stood up angrily. 'I told you there'd be trouble if you tried to marry Brett.'

'Not *try*,' Jay stormed in. 'I'm *marrying* Brett.'

'There's a little time left!' yelled Kerri.

Morton no longer bothered to conceal his disgust.

'Get Kerri's things together, Elaine,' he said in a commanding tone of voice.' I'm taking her home.'

Brett went with Jay out into the night. She didn't know how much more of it she could have taken.

CHAPTER SEVEN

THE following day Brett received a visit from Elaine. Mrs Chase was not at home. She had a morning appointment with her doctor, a routine check, and afterwards she planned to have lunch with two of her dearest friends.

'I saw the Rolls go by,' Elaine offered, when Brett went to answer the door chimes. 'May I speak to you?'

'No arguments, Elaine. I couldn't stand it.'

'No arguments,' Elaine agreed wryly. 'Morton and I have been at it for hours. I didn't realise he could get so angry! If he would give himself half a chance, he'd be quite a guy.'

'A strange thing to say of your husband?' Brett led the way to the garden room with its plumply upholstered wicker chairs and dazzling array of indoor plants.

'Morton has always walked in someone's shadow—J.B.'s, that terrible man, his brother, Jay. Maybe he can never measure up to Jay in terms of brilliance, but he's bright enough.'

'He'd even do better if you'd allow him to be his own man.'

For a moment Elaine couldn't find her own voice. 'For a cool little thing you don't pull your punches!' she snapped.

'I care about Morton—at least I would if he'd let me. I know how Morton suffered.'

'I guess it wasn't your fault at that.' Elaine slumped into a chair.

'Coffee?'

'And lots of it. I have a hangover. Don't I look it close up?'

'I've never known you look anything else but good.' Brett turned her shining dark head. 'Ah, there you are, Mrs Harris. Do you think we might have coffee?'

'Certainly,' the housekeeper said. 'Good morning, Mrs Carradine.'

Elaine nodded pleasantly and waited for the housekeeper to move off. 'I haven't been very nice to you, have I, Brett?'

'Obviously you felt you didn't like me.' Brett stopped to cup the flower of a magnificent pink amaryllis, then sat down opposite her visitor.

Elaine shrugged. 'That wasn't it. J.B. did so much damage. I've even come around to thinking he was cruellest to you even when he made such a fuss over you. There were all those stories when you were a child, he could have stopped them. It was a crime really, and you got caught in the middle.'

'It's too late now,' Brett said wryly. 'Everyone has a theory why J.B. did as he did. Only the poor have to obey the rules. Men as rich as J.B. did as they liked. It's a way of life.'

'Well—I don't dislike you, Brett.' Elaine's voice was very dry and brittle. 'I admire you, as a matter of fact. And I was very upset to hear what happened last night.'

'You mean with Kerri?'

Elaine hesitated. 'I know this won't go any further, but Kerri rather forced me to go along with her. We go back a long way. Kerri's great as long as you don't cross her—in that respect she's like her old man. She urged me to help her with the photographs—a fellow called Joe Campigli took them. Jay can trace anything when he tries. Kerri was counting on your not showing them to him. I'm not pleased with what I did. Morton is shocked.'

'You got caught?' There was a note of humour in Brett's voice.

'Shocked that I tried to upset his brother.'

There was a rustling sound as Mrs Harris returned and Brett stood up and took the tray. 'Thank you. That looks lovely.'

Elaine sat back in her chair. 'Do you think you could get me some aspirin, Mrs Harris? My head is pounding!'

'I'm sorry—I'll get some right away.'

Brett looked at Elaine's strained face. 'You don't have to explain any more. Relax.'

'I can't relax until I get it over. Anyway, Morton is frantic for you to know I had no idea what Kerri was up to last night. He kept me awake for hours after he came home. He used to like Kerri—or I thought he liked her—but he's gone off her now. He thinks she has no sense of pride.'

'Pride is difficult when one's in love. I don't think it strange she loves Jay. I expect if I marry him I'll have a problem all my life.'

'*If?* Don't you mean *when*?'

Mrs Harris loomed up again with the aspirin and Elaine swallowed them down. 'Shall I pour?' she asked.

'Thank you.' Brett accepted a little cake, but Elaine waved temptation away.

Mrs Harris went off, pleased to see such harmony. She had worked for the Chase family for thirty years and was as well acquainted with family matters as any one of them.

'The point *is*,' Elaine picked up the conversation, 'I want no more of this. I expect Kerri will give me a bad time. She might even divulge one or two things I'd rather be kept quiet. Your life is in *your* hands, Brett. I expect a lot has happened to you for such a young woman—all that money, Jay ... There couldn't be a woman alive who wouldn't go mad for Jay. To be frank, I made a play for him myself. We both know he's had quite a few affairs, but *you* were always different. Some people might think he's taking over where his father left off, but *I* think he loves you.'

'Why *me*?'

Elaine unexpectedly laughed, then winced as it hurt her head. 'I've never met anyone without vanity before. You're beautiful. Surely you know that?'

'If that's all Jay wanted he could have made up his mind long ago,' sighed Brett.

'Then doesn't that answer your question? Hell, even I know he's always been there for you. Obviously he's been waiting for you to grow up. Of course, it's much better now you're rich!'

Brett sat there for a long time after Elaine had gone. There was no gentle way to say it. Her inheritance had certainly brought Jay to the point.

The next time Brett entered the Carradine building she met David. She watched the colour flood his sunbrowned face. 'I think of you and what happens!'

She smiled and held out her hand. 'How are you, David? Jay told me you're the latest whizz kid in the legal department.'

'It's great. I'm settling in well.' His brown eyes, intelligent and warm, were transparent in their pleasure. 'How are *you*?' He broke off as a harassed business man bumped into him without apology and hurried off. 'Going up to see Jay?'

'I was.'

'I think you'll find he's completely tied up. There's been some sort of disaster. Nothing I'm sure Jay can't fix.'

'Why, what happened?' Brett allowed him to manoeuvre her into a quieter, safer place.

'None of us have the details yet. I know Jay was looking like thunder and telling Morton to get in on the double. Probably something poor old Mort's done.'

'Maybe I should go up?'

'Maybe you shouldn't,' David warned. 'At least, not for a half hour or so. I'm shooting out for a bite of lunch. I've been working on something long and tedious and I haven't had the chance yet. Why don't you join me for a cup of coffee? That way you'll miss the worst of the storm.'

Brett stood there, undecided. Finally she reasoned she would only be in the way if she went up to Jay. 'All right, that'll be nice.'

It was long past the recognised lunch break, so they had no wait. David ordered a crumbly butter-rich crab quiche and a salad, while Brett kept him company with coffee and a small slice of a spectacular gateau that tasted like chocolate velvet.

'I think I'll have to have some of that,' David remarked. 'You look beautiful, Brett, as always. Are you happy?'

Brett raised her delicate black eyebrows. 'Wait a second. Don't I look happy?'

'Being happy is a difficult matter. There seem to be shadows in those luminous eyes.'

'Maybe my eyeshadow is all wrong.' She kept the quizzical smile on her face. 'I'm happy, David. How could I not be? I'll be a married woman in a few weeks.'

'You don't think you ought to wait?'

'David, stop that! Jay is your boss!'

'And I want to say he's great, but you're so young!'

'Twenty-one on December the twentieth. I just missed out on being a Christmas baby.' I just missed out on a lot.

'I was wondering when I'd see you again,' David's brown eyes very nearly smouldered. 'I know I have no right to say that.'

'It's a little foolish, David,' Brett pointed out gently. 'It could be self-destructive.'

David's smooth skin reddened. 'To think I had to meet you now! Why not a year ago?'

Something in his expression moved Brett's tender heart and she stretched out her hand.

'David, it wouldn't have made the slightest difference. Jay's in my blood, in my bones.'

'God damn him,' muttered David, shaking his head.

'David, if you feel like that why ever did you accept a position within the Corporation? Where is your loyalty to Jay? I think loyalty is terribly important.'

'Of course it is,' he agreed seriously, putting down his fork. 'In our professional lives I'm loyal to Jay all right. I'd probably have to be certified crazy if I weren't. In fact Jay would find out immediately and sack me. I wouldn't care to cross him. I respect him as a person, as a boss. If anything, I'm like the rest of them—I grovel at his feet. The only thing I don't like about Jay is, he's got *you*.'

Brett was shocked. 'David,' she said finally, 'you make me nervous.'

'You know another funny thing?'

'Really, I don't think I want to know.' Brett felt like her coffee cup would fall from her fingers.

'I fell in love with you on sight.'

'It's a good thing that's so unreliable.' Agitation was flushing Brett's magnolia skin with wild colour. 'You don't know me, David. We're almost strangers.'

'That's just it—we're not. You don't feel strange with me. I don't feel strange with you.'

'David,' she said helplessly, 'I'm terribly embarrassed. I do like you, but I love *Jay*, remember?'

'I don't think Jay's right for you.'

'Surely *I* should decide.'

'Please don't be angry, Brett,' he begged her. 'I know I'm out of line, but I can't seem to help myself. You want a friend. You *need* a friend. I know you're without family. Sometimes there's a look in your eyes and I think, why, she's just a little kid. Getting married is an awfully big decision.'

'You would like to make it for me?' Brett gave a strange little laugh like a bell in her throat. 'David, I think we'll have to forget this conversation. You might want to work for the Corporation, but it could become impossible.'

'Oh, Brett, you'd never give me away,' he exclaimed ardently. 'You shouldn't be pressured into this thing.'

'And how do you know I *am*?'

David's eyes fell to his neglected lunch plate. 'People talk.'

'And *people* think I'm being pressured, do they?'

'Please, Brett,' he caught her fingers. 'All I think about is you. Whether Jay can make you happy. Women are crazy about him—lots of women. I've seen them throw themselves at him with my own eyes. It's understandable, I guess: he's as handsome as the devil and he's filthy rich. The thing is, women like that aren't going to care whether he gets married or not. They won't think of you. Especially not you. All they'll think of is what they can get out of him. One of the girls in the office brought her sister up just so she could get a look at him. I mean, I ask you! Probably it would be like being married to a movie star. Some goddamn sex symbol.'

'The only thing you've omitted,' Brett pointed out quietly, 'is that Jay doesn't even *see* the women who chase him and when he does, he gets intensely irritated. I think you're forgetting I've known him all my life. I've seen the same things you have. I've seen how Jay reacts. He's thirty-two and I can tell you he doesn't fall in love easily.'

'Can you swear he's in love with *you*?'

Brett stood up with calm dignity and gathered up her soft leather handbag. 'A real friend, David, would not say these things to me. A loyal employee of the Carradine Corporation would never allow themselves to become trapped in such a situation.'

'Brett, forgive me.' David jumped up, a muscle beside his mouth working. 'I *am* your friend, believe me. I would do anything for you. *Anything*. Just ask me.'

'Why don't you, darling?' a voice asked behind them, and both Brett and David broke off in a shocked panic.

Kerri Whitman's face popped around the side of the adjoining high-backed banquette.

David swore. A thick vein stood out on his forehead. Brett felt sick with disgust.

'I suppose you've been deliberately listening!'

'Sure have.' Kerri stood up. 'Would you like me to play it back? Really, David, you ought to have your head examined. When I send this to Jay,' she turned her head to indicate some device, 'your career is over.'

'But you're not interested in David, are you? You're only interested in me. And I doubt very much if you walk around with a micro-recorder in your bag. Though all things are possible.' Brett made a swoop and in front of Kerri's outraged eyes emptied her handbag out on the table.

'How *dare* you!' Kerri who exulted in laying traps bitterly resented being a victim.

'Please—it's quite all right.' Brett rummaged through the assortment of objects on the table, exactly the sorts of things a woman usually carried in her handbag. No recording device of any kind.

'Tell me, you weren't here when we arrived. Did you go past the window and nearly fall over?' she asked Kerri.

'As a matter of fact, I did.' Kerri slumped down

in the banquette. 'The two of you were so engrossed in each other you didn't even see me. I've never heard such rubbish! Just how did you think you were going to work for Carradine and doublecross Jay?' she asked David bitterly. 'You're so awfully nice, aren't you? A cut above me. Yet you're prowling around Jay's precious little half-sister.'

'You're disgusting, Kerri,' Brett said scornfully. 'It's the only thing you seem to understand.'

'If I can make trouble for you, I *will*!'

Kerri looked so white and wretched Brett passed a hand before her eyes. 'Please, David, sit down. Mercifully the restaurant is almost empty, but even then Jay will get a report back. Kerri,' she sat down beside the older woman, 'do you think I'm so insensitive I can't feel your pain? I know you're in love with Jay, but it's time you went after a little help. He's not in love with you. I doubt if he could be barely civil to you these days. What you're doing is very foolhardy and it will become a matter of grave concern for your family if you persist.'

Kerri laughed harshly. 'I no longer try to follow you, Brett. If anyone tried to take my man I'd kill her!'

'Then aren't you really saying Jay *isn't* your man? You *know* he isn't. Please try to leave your emotions aside and think this out. So you had a rapport? There have been other women in Jay's life. Remember Sally Grosvenor?'

'Yes, I do, boring creature.'

'She rated pretty high with Jay. She was very kind to me.'

'Have you ever thought that's why?' There was a kind of anguish in Kerri's hazel eyes. 'I lost Jay the moment you grew up.'

'I'm so sorry,' Brett said.

'The incredible part is I believe you are, but that changes nothing. Without you everything would be different.'

All at once Brett could see it was useless. Kerri had withdrawn beyond help. 'Please don't make trouble, Kerri,' she begged.

'If you imagine I'm going to let that snake off the hook. I'd do anything for you, Brett—*anything*,' she mimicked David with extravagant scorn.

'Isn't it a little bit like what *you're* doing?' Brett asked quietly. 'I might be a curious person, but I can only feel pity for people in love. It's the same for everybody, the brilliant and the ordinary, the rich and the poor. Sometimes I think it could be treated as a disease. No one seems to have any control over what they're doing. You're a confident, glamorous woman, yet a pathetic jealousy has taken you over. David is considered a brilliant legal brain, yet he's caught in some fantasy about me. I can barely remember a moment of my life without Jay. Keeping us together seems to be first on Jay's list of priorities. He's determined to marry me. What else can I say—to both of you? You may beat me down, but how are you going to beat Jay?'

'Well, I'm going to have a damn good try,' Kerri gave a harsh laugh. 'It's all very well for you to play the real lady, but ladies usually wind up getting crushed.'

The street outside was filled with people, light and the rumbling sounds of traffic. 'I'm through,' David said bleakly. 'For years I've been working towards this kind of job, and now I've messed it up.'

'She mightn't say a thing,' Brett pointed out.

'I don't think you understand Kerri Whitman's kind of woman. She's been utterly cruel about you, yet you show her sympathy.'

'She needs it,' Brett told him soberly.

'I don't think there's any chance she won't use what she thinks she's got on us both.'

'Then I'll deny it,' Brett decided. 'Kerri seems to think I won't lift a finger to help myself, but she's quite wrong. Of course what I'm trying to do is help *you*. You'll get over this, David—this little infatuation. It's a passing thing. You're working towards a long and satisfying career.'

'I'd place *you* first.'

'Oh, David!' Brett didn't feel she could take any more. 'Can't you see you're setting yourself up for disaster?

'And no more able to help myself than Kerri Whitman,' David agreed wryly. 'You don't need Jay's permission to have coffee with me. Kerri's a woman who's made lots of trouble. There's a good chance Jay mightn't believe her. I don't intend to drop out of the organisation until I'm fired.'

He was fired the same day.

Brett knew it from one furious, blazing look.

'What the hell does he think he's doing around here?' Jay propelled Brett into his office, towering over her.

'I met him downstairs. We had a cup of coffee.'

'Just like that?' Jay laughed. It sounded menacing and dangerous. 'I gave him credit for more damned sense. Did he actually think he could step on my toes? I could swat him into oblivion like a mosquito.'

'It sounds like overkill.'

'Sit down, Brett,' ordered Jay. 'I'm not coming down hard for nothing. I saw all the moon-eyed looks back on Diamond Valley. Of course I'm a reasonable man; I'm even a tolerant one. I gave him a chance. You do inspire a compulsive idiocy.'

'Thank you.' Brett threw up her dark head. 'Mercifully you don't suffer from it.'

'It's disloyal, Brett,' he said harshly. 'It's disloyal and it's underhand.'

'And who says? Kerri Whitman?'

'Brett,' Jay rasped grimly, 'I'm extremely harassed today. I'll get around to that in time. Kerri did manage to get through to me, posing as her mother. She had quite a story.'

'And you believed her?' Brett asked feelingly.

'You bet your life I did!' The jagged mockery of his tone cut through to her heart. 'Kerri's a born provocateur on the one hand, but I've been doing some observing myself. Dave's so far gone he thinks nothing of pursuing a girl who's damn near at the altar. That's bad enough, but how about this? He *works* for me. I offered him a job—a good job. The chance to go as high as he likes. But it seems that's inadequate weighed against you.'

'Kerri's lying.' Brett spread her hands. They were very pretty hands: small, fine-boned, long-fingered. The sapphire was as clear and blue as some wonderful subterranean grotto, the surrounding diamonds blazed in the light.

'Look at me, Brett.' Jay sounded very severe.

She lifted her head, the colour racing under her beautiful skin. 'It was all quite innocent, I assure you.' At least she might save David's career.

'Do you imagine I can't read your eyes? I know everything about you.'

She gave a muffled little exclamation and leapt to her feet. She put out her hand and gripped his wrist. 'Please don't fire David,' she begged.

'Pleading, are you?' His eyes, as blue as her sapphire, slanted over her unpleasantly.

'How could David hurt *you*?' Brett pleaded.

'My dear Marisa, it appears he's having a damned good try. When have you ever pleaded for me? Your eyelashes are all wet.'

'Jay, I'm asking you,' she said with soft poignancy.

'And the answer is David is getting his walking papers today.' His brilliant eyes glittered under their lids. 'I can accept an unwilling attraction. I cannot accept sabotage.'

'But *I* have to accept it from Kerri.' Now Brett's silvery eyes filled right up with tears. 'I have to accept lots of things, whereas you accept nothing.'

'That's right. He caught her delicate shoulders.' 'Anyone who tries to get to you answers to me. Finally it seems someone went directly to Gunn at Westlake and informed him of our intentions.'

Brett heard what he was saying, but for a moment couldn't take it in. 'Westlake,' she repeated.

He prodded her memory bluntly. 'Don't tell me you've forgotten our recent Board meeting?'

'So what has it to do with me?'

'Maybe Dave decided he wanted you and an alternative career?'

'I'm sure nothing could be further from his mind!' Brett looked and sounded shocked. 'Why is

David the only one you've thought of?'

'Surely I wouldn't think of *you*.'

'*What!*' She looked up at him in amazement and distress.

'It has been suggested to me.'

'Morton?' Her sensitive face was shadowed with pain.

'Morton, my dear, is sufficiently on your side to write that sick suggestion off. You have one hell of an aura, Brett, but no one who knows you would ever accuse you of double dealing. You're incapable of treachery. My brother and I know perfectly well you had nothing to do with it. The suggestion was very neat—too neat. Some people seem to go out of their way to set themselves up for a fall. David Cooper is one of them.'

'David didn't do it,' Brett shook her head.

'David Cooper has done enough.' Jay's hand closed under her chin. 'He's no one to cry about.'

'If you sack him I promise I——'

'*What?*' His hard fingers pinched.

'*Please* don't sack him, Jay,' she begged.

There was a cold hostility in his eyes, an arrogant set to his handsome head. He looked incredibly like J.B.

'No one—but no one—plays me for a fool. Cooper goes.'

The leak led to an intensive inquiry, but no one asked Brett any more questions.

Elaine, on the other hand, was distraught. 'You've got to help me, Brett,' she whispered over the phone. 'I just don't know how this thing will finish.'

Brett invited her up to the house so they could talk—about what, Brett didn't know. Surely Elaine couldn't have had anything to do with it? Elaine was a woman who worked untiringly in what she saw to be her husband's interests. The engagement party was scheduled for the following Saturday night. Brett found, even with help, there was a great deal to do. She hoped what Elaine had to say wouldn't take long. She still had a last fitting for her dress, which was being made by a top designer. It was a black tie occasion and Brett realised she would be very much on show. It was almost impossible to jam all the things she had to do in.

'Thanks a lot for seeing me,' Elaine burst out in a rush. 'I know how busy you must be. Incidentally, if there's anything I can do please let me know. Gran in?'

Brett nodded. 'She's resting in her room. She says she wants to be at her best on Saturday night.'

'She has always favoured you. I could turn into an angel, but it wouldn't make any difference. I know she doesn't think a great deal of me.'

'That's not true, Elaine,' Brett glanced at her quickly.

'Oh, don't worry, I can see you're embarrassed. Gran takes a very strict view of certain things, and I know I haven't come up to scratch.'

'I know you would do anything for Morton's sake,'

'Gran thinks I'm a bad influence in his life.' Elaine sat down.

'Not a *bad* influence, Elaine—scarcely that. Maybe she thinks Morton is more capable than you allow. He affects that very casual style as a cover.

He's really a man of brain '

'In the man of brawn?'

'Jay tells me repeatedly that Morton is blooming,' said Brett.

'Now J.B.'s gone?'

'J.B. *was* the major influence on Morton's life. While Jay fought him at every turn, Morton's way was to conform. A lot of people thought he would simply collapse, but in fact Jay has given him the one thing he lacked— direction. Jay's very clever with people. More importantly, he loves his brother.'

'I *know* that, Brett,' Elaine agreed, meekly for her. 'If Jay is the ideal, *my* husband is proving he's no mediocrity. Foolishly I thought Jay might shove him into the background. I *really* thought that. So did Dad. We didn't see anything between J.B. and Jay. We didn't see all the decency. J.B. never looked on Morton indulgently in his whole life. Jay pushes his brother further and further on. You could say Dad and I were J.B.'s dupes. We thought after he had gone Jay would take his place. Even Dad had to admit it showed our poor judgment, and that's quite a thing for *my* father to admit. Jay has backed his brother all along. Belatedly I realise that for the past few years I've been doing all the wrong things. Morton talks wistfully about a family. I've sought to keep up my social life and my figure. You more than anyone have made me feel a poor thing.'

'But what have *I* done, Elaine? I'm grappling with my own problems.'

'You've got something that Gran's got—a kind of high-mindedness, a disdain for anything dirty or underhand,' Elaine explained.

'I can't imagine your doing the things I've done. You came out of that business with Kerri with dignity, although she can't accept that she can't be the winner. It's Kerri I want to talk to you about now.'

'She's not on the move again, is she?' Brett asked dismally.

Elaine lit a cigarette and exhaled a great gust of smoke. At Brett's age she had been a picture of glowing prettiness, but her model-girl aspirations and later the right sort of clothes had set her on the path of smoking to alleviate her hunger pangs. Now she gestured furiously.

'I don't care what she does to me. This whole thing is getting me down—I can't sleep, I'm drinking too much and I smoke one cigarette after another.'

'Why don't you give it all away and have a baby?' Brett said suddenly. 'You're not happy, Elaine, the way you are. I don't like to see you abusing your body. All those cigarettes are really bad. I won't bore you by going on, but obviously you're now thinking of starting a family. You *couldn't* smoke if you were pregnant.'

'I wouldn't.' Abruptly Elaine put her cigarette out. 'My mother is always at me too. The thing is, Brett, when Kerri and I were friends . . .'

'You're not now?'

Elaine laughed. 'I guess we were never friends. I have to re-read the whole book. Kerri and I were bosom buddies, or so I thought. Actually our friendship wasn't all that bad. It was a lot of fun. We obviously did what we liked.' She swallowed and gave a pathetic, shamefaced grin. 'Once when

Morton was away I had a bit of a——'

'You don't have to tell me, Elaine. Your affairs are your own.'

'You have to know what this is about,' insisted Elaine. 'It seems very remote now, a passing aberration, but Kerri reminds me of it every so often. The implied threat is that she would tell Morton. He would never understand—Morton is that extraordinary thing, an entirely faithful husband. I want you to believe this, Brett. It's most important that you do. In passing I happened to mention to Kerri that we were planning the Westlake take-over,' she added.

'Oh, my God!' Brett cried expressively, instantly seeing the rest.

'Brett.' Elaine grabbed her hand. 'I never thought for one moment Kerri would repeat it, let alone pass on the story. It just popped out as things sometimes do. I'd been telling Kerri things for years and years. It was as if she was my sister. Kerri has never done anything to hurt any one of us.'

'Until now .'

Elaine pulled out a handkerchief and dabbed her eyes vigorously. 'Oh, Brett, what am I to do? I'm terrified of Jay. Sometimes I don't know who he is. He can look so much like J.B. All that charm turns to a kind of caged ferocity.'

'It was a mistake, an indiscretion,' Brett began.

'If Gran knew she would detest me for life.'

'You meant no harm, Elaine,' Brett said in a worried voice. 'Was it Kerri who went to Westlake?'

'I don't know precisely if it was Kerri. It was Kerri who set up the meeting. She boasted about it.

The incredibly foolish part was she thought it would reflect on *you*.'

'But Jay knows me,' Brett pointed out dryly.' Anyway, I'm on the Carradine Board. Why would I work against my own interests?'

'To spite Jay.'

'My God, how extraordinary! I'm afraid Kerri Whitman has too devious a mind.'

'Be sure of it,' Elaine groaned. 'Do you think you could possibly go to Jay? I'm so madly upset. If Morton was to know! I think he'd probably divorce me.'

'Why don't you tell him everything and set the record straight?'

'I can't, Brett,'Elaine said simply. 'Would *you* like to tell Jay you'd had an affair? If you couldn't tell him now how do you think you'd tell him if you were married?'

Brett grimaced. 'But if there's the possibility that Kerri would tell Morton anyway, wouldn't it be better if he heard it from you?'

'There's a chance he won't hear it at all if you got to Jay. Jay's the great fixer.'

'He may already know.'

Elaine moaned miserably. 'If he does, he hasn't told his brother.'

'Telling wouldn't be Jay's way. You might be hurt, but equally so would Morton.'

'Could you speak to Jay for me, Brett?' Elaine begged. 'I swear, I *swear* my indiscretion was entirely innocent. It never occurred to me at that time Kerri would do anything with the information.'

'I can try, Elaine,' Brett promised.

'You're a pal!'

'Whatever is happening to Elaine these days?' Mrs Chase asked afterwards. 'Didn't I see her kiss you when she left this morning? I happened to be looking through my window—the roses are glorious—and there was Elaine acting like a real woman for a change!'

What Elaine did not realise was that relations between Brett and Jay were strangely taut. Engagement parties, weddings were going on, but the atmosphere between them was electric.

Brett rang Jay's office and when she got through to him he sounded very crisp and businesslike. She had to choke back an answering briskness and asked him quite sweetly would he mind calling in to see her.

'Better still, I'll call and pick you up,' he told her.

'You don't have to bother to . . .'

'Got it?' he asked bluntly, and hung up.

He arrived about six-thirty, spent some time with his grandmother who was delighted to see him, then escorted Brett down the wide, shallow stone steps to his car.

'This *is* an honour, Marisa,' he said with something of his brother's easy drawl. 'I do like that dress—such a beautiful colour. What would you call it, jacaranda?'

'Jacaranda, lavender-blue, deep mauve, any of those.'

'Hungering for my company, are you?'

Brett's temper was rising, but she had sense enough to try and turn his hard mockery aside. 'Surely I can call the man I'm going to marry in a little over a week?'

'I'm so glad you remember,' he drawled.

'I do.'

He stopped before he pulled out the gates. 'You just listen to me, little one. There's going to be no fool contract between us. I've treated you like a piece of precious jade. All I've allowed myself is a few reverent strokes. On our wedding night, you're *mine*.'

She seemed to recoil. In reality her whole body came so shudderingly alive she had to arch back against the contoured seat.

'Whatever's in your mind, forget it. Just be grateful I've appreciated your youth and your innocence so far.' Jay pulled the gear lever into drive and the Jaguar took off with velvet smoothness. 'You'll be twenty-one, my wife, and if it's any consolation I promise I'll make you a great lover.'

'Then why do I get the impression you'd like to beat me?'

He looked at her and laughed. 'I thought you said, eat you. There's a better thought. Have I ever actually struck you?'

'Yes,' she said. 'At least, you shook me and called me a stupid little twit.'

'And when was this?' Amusement softened the hard handsomeness.

'I was inside one of the horse stalls, and you thought I'd been kicked at first.'

'I didn't know then that you and horses were on such friendly terms,' Jay said drily. 'Where do you want to go for our honeymoon?'

'Really, you're *asking* me?'

'I'd get a lot more pleasure out of being given your preferences. You're very unusual, Brett, for a fiancée.'

'Perhaps I've never felt like one?'

'You'd feel like one if you ever tried to get away.'

They stopped at a red light and Jay glanced down at his watch. 'Where would you like to go for dinner?'

'Somewhere different. Somewhere where everyone doesn't know you're the great Jay Carradine.'

'Also, they don't know *you*. You've been getting yourself in the social pages lately. You take a great photograph.'

'So do you.'

Dinner was spiced with the same kind of barbed banter. Brett kept her end up very well, but inside she cringed from approaching the subject of the Westlake leak. Also one bad experience precluded ever discussing deeply personal or sensitive matters in a restaurant again.

'So what is it you've been mulling over all through dinner?' Jay asked as they were leaving.

She could scarcely control a little sigh. 'How do you know there was anything on my mind?'

'You're nervous and you don't really want to talk about it.'

'I'm glad that's over.'

He put her into the car and came around the other side.

'Are you sure you have the right address?' Brett asked as they turned towards the city.

'I'm not taking you home yet, Marisa.' He moved out to overtake a slow-moving taxi. 'So anyway, what's bothering you?'

'I don't think I can face it without a stiff drink.'

'*That* bad?'

She nodded. 'I'll tell you when we get to the penthouse. If things get awkward, I can always jump!'

Brett was deeply conscious of the quiet of the penthouse. Unlike Diamond Valley or even the Chase mansion, no magnificent chandeliers were appended from the ceilings. Jay's designer had created a miracle of modern lighting where the whole system was virtually hidden yet created myriad effects. There were lights on the pictures, and these with one or two others brought drama and mystery to the large L-shaped room. It was a study in gold and black and crimson, and Brett felt her heart begin to flutter in a strange fear and excitement.

She sank down into one of the soft, rich banquettes and fervently closed her eyes. It was safer than following Jay's every move. His body spoke to her. Every lithe movement. He was so much a part of her she couldn't exorcise him for a minute.

He must have touched a switch, because music insinuated itself seductively into the atmosphere. Brett recognised the work: Stravinsky. It wrapped its way around her senses, the throb and thrum of the strings touching chords deep within her. Music very often reduced her to tears. For years, instead of human companionship, she had only had music and her beloved horses to turn to. They had never let her down.

She shivered and her eyes flew open when Jay ran a finger down her cheek. 'Why the poignant expression?'

She turned her head to look up at him. 'I was just

thinking of the things that have always given me pleasure.'

'It's only right and proper that music should be one of them. It even releases *my* demons.'

'Well, I'll allow you a few,' she sighed.

'Want that drink now?'

'I'm no drinker, Jay.'

'I know that, but you told me you needed some Dutch courage.'

'Are you going to sit down or are you going to prowl around the room?' she sighed.

'I *can't* sit beside you.' Jay's vibrant voice was low and mocking.

'Why not?' It came out as a little gasp.

'Well, I'm not all that near to you now and you're trembling. I can almost feel the flutter of your heart.'

'What I have to tell you won't make you happy.' She didn't look at him as she said this, so she didn't see the sudden glitter in his eyes.

'So long as you don't tell me you plan to ditch me at the altar?'

'No, nothing like that,' Brett shook her cloudy dark head. 'It's about Westlake . . .' she trailed off.

'I wouldn't think of discussing that now.' Jay shed his jacket and stripped off his silk tie. 'If you aren't going to have a drink, join me in a mineral water.'

Brett appeared to be oblivious to his refusal. 'You've said things in confidence, Jay, that you never intended to be repeated?'

'What I don't intend to be repeated I don't pour into irresponsible ears.'

'Won't you please come and sit down?'

'Certainly, darling. Alongside you. But be sure my behaviour will be pure and wholesome. I may be scorching inside, but I have to wait until my wedding before I gain possession of my so beautiful bride. You will allow me on our wedding night, won't you, Marisa? I think I'd better start getting some guarantees that I'll be allowed access to the marital bed.'

'Jay, this isn't any joking matter!' she protested.

He sat down so close to her, Brett slipped her feet out of her elegant evening pumps and drew her legs under her.

'Won't you crush your dress?' His sapphire eyes slid satirically over her arching, slender body.

'It's uncrushable. Or almost.' She recognised his sardonic mood and it didn't bode well for her.

'Why don't I just put you out of your misery?' he said coolly. 'I won't allow Cooper back into Carradine, but I spoke up for him with Hall, Mackenzie. Gavin's a very discreet man. I had to tell him something close to the truth, otherwise they would have questioned why I sacked him. I guess even a man can understand love, or more explicitly, infatuation. Cooper couldn't stay with us any longer; that would be continually feeding the flames.' He swept his blue eyes over her. 'Satisfied, little one? You won't think me a beast?'

'You mean you saw to it that David got a job?' She leant forward, her smoky eyes soft and melting.

He stirred somewhat impatiently, his handsome face tight. 'Why shouldn't I respond to your piteous little pleas? I can please you there if nothing else.'

'Oh Jay!' she sighed, and put her head on his shoulder. 'As far as David is concerned I'm very

pleased. I know he was foolish, but the oddest
things happen. He was drawn to me, and I didn't
know.'

'Shouldn't you forget it now?'

She put her arms around him. 'Thank you.'

'Strange how someone else can inject a little
warmth!' mused Jay.

'What do you mean?' Brett lifted her head and
stared into his eyes. They were very close. She only
had to move an inch and she could brush her mouth
against his bronze, polished skin. He had very fine
white teeth and the edges of his handsome mouth
were slightly uplifted and cleanly delineated. She
could almost taste its texture.

'What are you staring at?' he asked crisply.

'You.'

'You must want something else?'

'I do.' Her sigh was a tiny sound at the back of her
throat. 'I don't want to bring this up all over again,
but I have to. I promised Elaine.'

'Elaine?'

There was so much disgust, incredulity, both, in
his tone, Brett tightened her hands together.

'I'll have to keep remembering I'm twenty-one in
a little over a week. Twenty-one means one is all
grown up. I have things to say and I'm going to say
it. I'm frightened.'

'What the hell!' Jay looked at her intensely. 'Your
face *is* white.'

'I don't think you know how really intimidating
you can be.'

'What—to you? I can't accept that, Brett.' He
sounded angry.

'Well, I fight very hard not to show it.'

'What?' It was said so sharply she might have jabbed him with a knife.

'You've had to be tough, Jay.'

'What, whips and all that?' Arrogance burned in his eyes.

'I know you've been good to me. J.B. was good to me, but I've told you, you have a very powerful aura. It's been strengthened over the years. Elaine was afraid to speak to you . . .'

'*Elaine* was afraid to speak to me,' he cut her off. 'Now you've got me really curious! Elaine has been handing me a line for years—it's her nature. What's she done now? Played up when Mort was out of town?'

Brett decided to speak out. 'In an unguarded moment she let slip to Kerri Whitman that the Board were thinking of taking over Westlake. She meant it in the strictest confidence, of course. She and Kerri Whitman have been friends for years, but Kerri decided to use it against you. *Me*, I suppose. She thought you would blame me and your anger would drive us apart.'

Jay sat and stared at her as though he couldn't speak.

Brett's tongue came out and explored her top lip. 'Jay?'

He stood up and walked through the sliding glass door to look out at the star-studded night. After a moment Brett decided to follow him, very small without her high-heeled evening shoes.

They stood together looking out over the dazzling lights of the city. Finally, Jay spoke. Brett had been expecting a fierce wrath, but instead his voice was cool and dry. 'It seems our dear Elaine spilled the beans for nothing. *You* happened to say to me that you didn't altogether trust our informant from Westlake, and it's not my way to trust informers either, though they do come up with highly classified information. Our informant was working both sides. By the time I'd finished with him he let it all out. I then went to Westlake and proposed a deal—a deal I expect they will take. Kerri Whitman's name was never mentioned. I've already spoken to her father as I knew I would have to. Kerri is going to have to work herself out overseas. I expect what she threatened Elaine with was nonsense. She's not such a fool as you all think. Trying to undermine Carradine would be like declaring war. Whi-Tec would never hand us *that* piece of paper. Kerri was lying, trying to frighten you. You should have come to me at once.'

'You mean Kerri meant it as a sick joke? That she never went to Westlake at all?'

Jay smiled unpleasantly. 'My dear, you need to toughen up yourself. I told you, Kerri wouldn't be such a fool. In hurting me she would only be hurting her father and brother, and that's something she would never do. I've another piece of information for you and Elaine,' he added. 'Kerri has already left for Hong Kong. She intends flying on to the U.K. and Europe. With any luck at all she might find herself a husband. She'll only have to mention that her family own one of the largest sheep stations in the country—the Golden Fleece and all that.'

Brett turned away quickly. 'She might have been kinder to her friend. Elaine was quite frantic!'

'Good. I hope it cures her entirely. Important

business matters shouldn't come into casual conversation. Even Mort is frightened of talking in his
sleep.'

Brett said nothing but returned inside. She
picked up her shoes, then sat down to put them on.

'Where do you think you're going?'

Jay spoke so tautly a cold tendril of panic writhed
through her. 'Aren't you taking me home? You
work so hard I wouldn't want to rob you of sleep.'

'Don't ride me hard, Brett,' he warned.

'It's just everyone is so *cruel*,' she cried emotionally. 'It seems I've never known anything but cruelty
all my life!'

'Strong words indeed!' He seemed to turn into a
panther, so with a quake of fear, she saw him lunge
and she became a victim in his arms. His eyes were
blue and blazing, the golden light glanced off his
high cheekbones. 'When was *I* ever cruel to you?'
He tilted her head back, catching her silky hair in
his hand. 'You should say a prayer, lady, that I was
around.'

'No, no, not you, Jay,' she moaned.

'Are you going to deny me your mouth?' He
shifted his hand and gripped her chin, his hard male
sensuality unleashed and roaming free.

She could only look at him. She couldn't speak.
At the centre of his eyes was a flame. Abruptly he
brought her body so close up against him she felt
weightless, liquid, her blood running molten. She
knew she gave a little cry as his encircling arms
turned to steel, then her lashes fluttered like dark
wings against her cheeks as his head came down
over hers.

She was taken over. Mastered. Jay's exclusive

possession.

The moment his mouth covered hers her slender body expelled all strength. Her soft weight pressed against him and recognising her weakness he picked her up like a mere doll.

Night surrounded them, enchanting music that rose and fell. Brett trembled on the edge of surrendering up her heart. Desire stabbed through her like an actual agony. She, who was incapable of putting voice to her passion, was wild for this hard ravishment to go on.

'What are you wishing for—a gentler lover?' Jay's handsome face was darkened with hot blood. 'David Cooper, maybe? You're no wife for him.'

He strode into the bedroom and threw her on to the wide bed. 'I know how you think of me, Marisa—a tyrant like my father. You think I'll take all you have to offer and give nothing in return. You think I'll try to subjugate you like J.B. did your mother. You think I'm only marrying you because you've now got the money to further my ambitions. You think I'm incapable of love, only lust. If that were indeed so I could have taken you at fifteen. You were raised thinking a woman was no more than a man's property. I would have thought a higher education would have set you straight, but you're still locked up in the old nightmares. You've had plenty of time, but you still fail to realise *I am not my father*! The old king is dead. I'm *me*, and I ache for some tenderness from you. You plead for someone like Cooper, and though it's against my own judgment I make sure he gets a second chance. You even plead for Elaine who is given you hell over the years. Now I have to listen to you telling me I'm too damned tough by far. So I terrify you, do I?'

'Please, Jay, I didn't say that,' she whispered.

'Take off that dress.'

Brett put her hand up to her throat. 'Jay, I . . . I can't . . . I wanted . . .'

'Take it off,' he repeated curtly. 'I don't want to ravish you, my darling, I simply want to pay court to your beauty. You have a slip underneath, haven't you? I have some idea how chaste you are, Marisa. That impenetrable reserve.'

She stared at him in bewilderment, but he turned away from her and walked to a vivid, abstract painting that hung above a magnificent brassbound Korean chest. The painting swung out and now Brett could see it masked a wall safe. Jay put his hand in and extracted a long velvet-covered case. Brett had seen it before. It housed the diamond and sapphire suite she had been told she would receive on her wedding day. Obviously Jay intended to see her in them now.

'Well?' He began to walk back to her, his smile twisted and caustic. 'Tremble all you want, but you have my word I'll keep my bargain to court you like a princess. A princess is expected to reserve her body.'

Brett lifted herself shakily off the bed. She put a hand to the top of the zipper at the back of her dress and pulled it down. The slip she wore beneath was the same beautiful jacaranda blue, designed especially for the gown it matched.

'Really, if I could kiss you the way I wanted, you'd be bruised all over!' muttered Jay.

She gave a little shiver, though the air was warm.

'Come here.' He held up the necklace and it glittered blue and ice fire. 'Jewels must be seen against skin,' he told her. 'Hail, Princess Marisa. You've achieved what's never been done before—you've brought me to my knees.' He turned her with one hand on her delicate shoulder and clasped the exquisite necklace around her long, slender throat. It felt cold and rather heavy, but he made her walk to the wall of mirrors in the adjoining dressing room.

Her slip dipped very low, the lace curved away to reveal the slight upper swell of her breasts. The gossamer thin material clung to her narrow torso, her waist, and slender hips. The lace hem hid her trembling knees. She should have looked ridiculous, but she looked incredibly erotic.

'Now the ear pendants,' Jay said briskly. He sounded for all the world like a jeweller making an important sale. 'No need to push your hair back, I like it all loose and cloudy. Well, perhaps just a little.' He flicked at a side curl. 'If I had to describe you, Brett, I'd say you were priceless. And consistent. Being consistent is very important. There!' He held her shoulders and stared at her. The top of her head came up to his shoulder. She was as white and slight as a geisha girl, but her silver glance could never have been mistaken for an invitation. She continued to look beautiful and stricken.

'I did intend giving these to you on our wedding day, but Gran tells me you've chosen blue for our engagement party. She thought it would be splendid if you wore the sapphires then. You should capture all hearts.'

'Are you done, Jay?' she asked quietly.

'I won't ask you for a grateful kiss, even though

I've had to be satisfied with the occasional kiss up to date. A lesser man would be howling.' His blue eyes were startling, as blue as the sapphires she wore at her breast.

'Thank you, Jay.' She looked down and touched the glowing stones while the pendants swung against her cheeks. 'I can't believe anyone would give me such a fabulous present. It makes me feel shaken inside.'

'So I'll settle for a smile. Isn't that how a princess behaves? A word here, a smile there. Always so gracious but never letting anyone know what goes on inside.'

'Don't be like this, Jay,' she entreated. 'I can't bear it. Why am I making you so angry? I try. I think I've been trying very hard.' Her voice broke.

'Don't cry,' he warned her with a half-blind impatience.

'Oh, *leave* me!' She tried to twist away, but as she did so his hand slipped over her shoulder and seemingly without his volition sought her naked breast.

The mirrored gesture was so sensual Brett thought she would faint. Her legs actually gave way, and he caught her under her narrow rib cage and pulled her back against him.

'Dear God!' he groaned. It was no blasphemy but a raw plea for help.

She began to cry, and quietly he gathered her up, jaw tight, nostrils flaring with the intensity of his feelings. In a daze she lay on the wide bed and he came to her, kissing her mouth, her face, her throat, the peaks and valleys of her breasts. His mouth, his hands, were so strong, so sure, so sensitive, her heart began to hammer in an excess of emotion. Her blue veins were trails of fire his fingertips set, and she began to allow him intimacies that went beyond anything she had known before.

Man was the true aggressor. It was a woman's nature to submit. Jay had a power over her impossible to withstand. It overwhelmed her with its force so that she didn't even know she was half-sobbing his name.

He lifted his head abruptly, staring down at her: white skin, japanned brows and lashes, rose satin mouth, tears like glittering diamonds spilling out towards her ears. Even the nipples of her small high breasts blossomed, suffused with colour from his touch. She looked drugged with ecstasy and a kind of virginal terror combined.

Jay never doubted he could take her then. She was so very young and vulnerable after all, immensely susceptible to him as she had always been. His palms slid across her satin skin and her eyes suddenly opened wide, settling dazedly on his dominant dark face, pale beneath its patina of golden bronze.

'I never meant to make you cry,' he said quietly, and smoothed back the gleaming hair that framed her face. 'I promised you I'd hold back and I will. God knows I've had to learn a powerful self-discipline.'

Her eyes were huge, glittering like ice crystals. Sapphires and diamonds gave off an unholy light. For the first time she truly realised what marriage with Jay would mean. A new dimension. Some fantastic world that altered space and time. Passion was a living, breathing entity. There were no theatricals to match it. Pleasure was so violent it had put her whole being into a sexual trance. Only Jay had stopped her surrender, though the planes of his face were as hard as a rock.

She tried, but she found she couldn't speak normally. Her voice was a mere whisper, her skin so translucent the light seemed to shine through it. 'Oh, Jay, what's going to happen when you find I'm not woman enough for you?'

'You're *not*?' His velvet voice was deep and sardonic.

'You must know I was nearly fainting now. Going right away.'

There was amusement in his brilliant eyes. 'Do *I* look so prosaic and solid?'

'You look very real and strong.'

'Well, I'm real enough,' he stroked around her ear. 'I don't know about strong. I'm waiting for my blood to subside. I made a pledge and I'm just going to have to keep it.'

'But what are you feeling about me?' Brett insisted desperately. 'There are so many secret places of the heart. I have nothing to go by. *Nothing*. I read books by the score. What do they tell me? Heroines tremble, they don't flake out.'

'It's a big world. Lots of different women in it.'

'I feel like a flame burning out of control.'

'Because, my dearest Marisa, you *are*.' There was a faint taunt buried in it. 'I shouldn't worry if you were going to be woman enough for me. Sooner or later you're bound to be too much!'

'I don't understand,' she faltered.

'Of course you don't,' he countered, rolling away and standing up. 'That's our problem.'

CHAPTER EIGHT

THERE were to be two celebrations—the actual ceremony and a grand reception in Adelaide, beautiful city of churches; another scheduled for Diamond Valley the day after. The Outback was not going to be deprived of the glorious opportunity to offer its congratulations to one of its most illustrious sons. Around two hundred people were expected to make the great trek to the historic station where they would set up camp like the pioneers of old.

Air Carradine was kept busy flying in the huge loads of provisions needed for such a celebration— it was expected to go on for days—and the household staff was augmented by well trained personnel including top caterers. The florist who had the huge commission of arranging the flowers for all three occasions had already jetted in and out to get an idea of what he wanted to see in the house, but the great banks of flowers, including the beautiful Queensland orchids, were to be delivered as late as possible to the station.

It was an exciting time and everyone became a trifle unhinged. Elaine, whose habitual manner was so laid-back it resembled a study in inertia, became astonishingly active. From opposing the marriage she now acted as though it had all been her idea.

'For goodness' sake, ask her to be matron of honour,' Mrs Chase suggested. 'I know it's *your* wedding . . .'

Brett, by nature a peacemaker, put the suggestion to Elaine very sweetly, and Elaine compulsively hugged her. One had to remember Morton was best man, after all.

'Dear God, how are we going to get through it?' Mrs Chase was heard to wail, but she, perhaps more than anyone, was filled with romance and excitement. She hadn't really taken to Elaine, so her elder grandson's marriage, though feverish, was untouched by the special aura she perceived in this wonderful occasion. Though she had never put it into actual words Jay had been her great favourite from the moment her daughter had placed him in her arms. He had waved at her—yes, he had actually *waved*. *That* story had been told, but to avoid complications Lillian Chase had never played favourites. One would have had to be a dyed-in-the-wool snob not to welcome Brett as one's own. She was as beautiful as a dream, and her character had the same classic harmony as her looks. Mrs Chase was well pleased.

The engagement part, in itself one of the social events of the year, gave a clue what the wedding would be. Brett couldn't remember much of it except that her beautiful, romantic dress had to be altered that very morning. The pace had become hectic, and though she was remembering to eat she was losing weight. The final touches on the master suite at Diamond Valley were still to be taken care of, and there were still a hundred and one things left to do.

As it was winter in the Northern Hemisphere, they had decided not to forsake the sun. There was all of the South Pacific to be explored, endless blue lagoons, palm trees and white sand. If they wanted to go shopping there was always Singapore and Hong Kong. The possibilities were all there to be decided on. What Brett really wanted was to come true. They would spend their wedding night at Diamond Valley, and old ghosts would be laid to rest.

Brett had asked her three closest friends from her university days to be her bridesmaids. They were thrilled to accept, and Brett immediately relieved them of all financial worry by explaining that Mrs Chase had insisted on paying for all the dresses, headpieces, Brett's veil and accessories. She had already assumed the position of grandmother to the bride.

'I know I'm not supposed to know what's going on,' Jay told her in one of the rare moments they had together. 'But I insist on a veil.'

'*You* want a veil?' Brett tried for lightness to balance her mounting tensions.

'No little hats, big hats, bows or whatever. I want a veil—a long veil. Tons of it. I want to throw it back and stare into your beautiful face. I've discovered I'm a very traditional man.'

Mercifully Brett had planned a veil all along. She had even decided on the romantic image Jay so plainly wanted. As a summer bride she felt the emphasis was on something delicate and cool, so she finally chose a beautiful embroidered white organza over strapless silk taffeta. The scalloped edge just touched her collarbones, the sleeves were big and billowy to match the full, romantic skirt and the waistline was small and tight. It was a young, very soft look, and it brought tears to Mrs Chase's eyes. The bridesmaids too were to wear embroidered organza in the same delicate shade of pink, the pink of the rosebuds planned for their bouquets and the circlet of pure silk flowers, pink and white, they were to wear on their heads. All three had thick, shining dark hair and varying shades of blue into green eyes, and the beautiful blush of pink colour suited them extremely well. Elaine had chosen something more sophisticated; a lovely gown featuring hand-made lace on Swiss voile with rose satin beneath. Brett hoped Jay would allow the elegant little pillbox hat their designer had devised. It was certain Elaine would not part with it. Almost as much time was spent deciding on Mrs Chase's outfit. She was as excited and exacting as the girls. There was something about weddings that brought out the young girl in everybody.

'Blue is always beautiful,' the designer suggested. 'Especially with blue eyes. I see a simple, very elegant flowing dress with a lace jacket. I know you have wonderful jewellery, Mrs Chase. Now the hat is important . . .'

So it went on until everything was perfected.

Brett could scarcely believe what had seemed like a dream from which she must surely wake was almost a reality. In a few days' time she was to marry Jay. A magnificent reception was planned. No one, however, said it was going to be a breeze. Both Jay and Brett were so pressured they scarcely found the time to communicate. Family and attendants were having all the fun. Jay couldn't even find the time for the church rehearsal, but Morton was too nervous about his role not to make it. Nothing was to go wrong. It was to be the wedding to end all weddings. The most sumptuous presents had arrived, so lavish Brett's eyes were dazzled. She had started life very differently from what it was now— and all because a rich and powerful man had desired her mother. He had never offered her the joy of marriage, yet Jay had chosen her daughter for his wife. The wheel had come full circle. Shouldn't she accept it?

The Chase mansion still retained three of its original ten acres and the reception for two hundred and fifty people was to be held in the house and the magnificent setting of the long established grounds. Brett was out in the garden watching one of the silk-lined marquees going up when she saw Elaine racing across the lawn, almost knocking into a stack of white garden chairs.

Brett knew immediately that something was wrong and her heart began to hammer in a fast-rising panic. She had never truly believed she could ever be so lucky. The gods had only briefly smiled on her before slamming her down.

Beads of nervous sweat stood out on Elaine's brow. She gestured frantically to Brett, calling her away from the scene of activity.

'What is it? What's wrong?' One look at Elaine's blanched face and a wave of nausea rose to Brett's throat.

'I've just come in,' Elaine waved a backward hand at her diamond-blue Mercedes parked along the drive. 'I just heard a newsflash. One of our helicopters is down. It crash-landed in the hills near the Hislop estate.'

Brett flinched.

'Oh, God, Brett,' the words expelled from Elaine in a violent rush, 'weren't Morton and Jay making a sweep of that area? I never pay attention, but I'm sure Morton said they were interested in buying acreage out there?'

'What did the bulletin say? Who was in it, who was hurt?'

'That's the only information they gave. A helicopter from the Carradine Corporation crash-landed in the hills. They'll have more information when it's to hand.' Elaine was almost babbling in her panic.

'It only takes a second to turn one's life upside down, 'Brett said strangely. 'I'm going out there. Right now.'

'There's the car. You'll have to drive—I can't.'

'We have to stop word of this getting to the house.' Brett started to move swiftly across the lawn.

'Gran could have a heart attack,' Elaine panted.

'We don't know *who* was in that helicopter,' Brett said grimly, surprised by the control she was keeping over her voice. 'We can only pray it wasn't Morton and Jay and that no one was badly hurt.'

Despite her shock and apprehension the Chase housekeeper assured Brett she would monitor all calls.

'Shouldn't I start making a few phone calls myself, Miss Brett?' she asked.

'It's just *happened*!' Elaine cried, so white she looked like a powdered and painted doll.

'We're going up there now,' Brett explained, grasping Mrs Harris's arm reassuringly. 'Take all calls, and whether the news is good or bad don't tell

Mrs Chase. You *must* wait for our return.'

'I understand, Miss Brett,' Mrs Harris promised soberly.

'I'm ill!' Elaine muttered as Brett turned out of the driveway and on to the road. 'It's just like some terrible nightmare. You never think anything is going to happen to you, to yours, then right out of the blue, just when everything is going right . . .'

Brett didn't answer. Life had made her a fatalist. She had lost father and mother; the man who had made her his ward. Her life had been a series of hard knocks, but if anything happened to Jay it might as well be over.

She pressed down harder on the accelerator and the powerful V8 engine responded with a deep-throated grunt. They were out of their beautiful garden suburb in the foothills and climbing towards the blue shimmering ranges. The needle hit 120, 140, 160k's.

'Brett, we'll be arrested!'

The car was performing brilliantly, revelling in a speed comfortably within its range. Brett's foot on the accelerator never slackened. It took a tremendous effort of control not to go faster. No policeman on a motor-cycle would stop her. She would go to jail if she had to, but first she had to get to Jay. It was too much of a coincidence that a Carradine helicopter was in the Hislop area. Unlike Elaine, she always listened. Jay was planning on securing a considerable holding in that district. One didn't need psychic powers to feel Jay and Morton had been in that helicopter.

They went a long way in a short time, when

terrifyingly they saw cars parked haphazardly
across a field. Two were easily distinguishable as
police cars, another wore the logo of a local T.V.
station, but the one their eyes were fixed on was the
bright yellow coronary unit.

'Don't worry about the car,' cried Elaine. 'Take it
over.'

It wasn't the kind of track the Mercedes coupé
was meant to ride. They went zigzagging cross-
country and now they could see the helicopter rising
out of a shallow depression.

'Brett!' In her agitation Elaine almost tore Brett's
arm from the wheel. 'It looks okay, doesn't it? I
don't see any . . . I don't see . . .'

Any bodies, Brett supplied grimly in her mind.

The uniformed policeman ran towards them,
waving his arms in a warning motion.

'Stop, Brett—you're supposed to *stop*!' Elaine
yelled.

'I'll stop when I get there.' For the first time in her
life Brett disobeyed a lawful signal. She swept on by
and jammed the car to a halt parallel to the
ambulance.

'Gosh, Brett,' Elaine exclaimed in awe, 'we might
be in trouble.'

'Who cares!' Brett's eyes were huge, the pupils
dilated. 'If anything has happened to either of them
our lives have come to a stop.'

They swung out of the car, leaving the doors
open. The policeman who had signalled them down
now advanced on them with a fellow officer, but
Elaine cried out in a loud voice,

'I'm Mrs Carradine . . . Carradine!'

Until then Brett had taken the initiative, but now

it suddenly seemed she was through. Some man in jeans and a pink shirt was trying to show Elaine a card, but she didn't even bother to read it. She raced towards the helicopter and disappeared down the slope.

'Please, miss . . .' Now the policeman was coming towards Brett. He was saying something, but she couldn't seem to catch it. There was a muffled sound in her ears as though she was swimming underwater. What did it matter anyway? There was no sign of Jay and the ambulance was empty.

'Amazing . . . simply amazing . . . I just don't know . . .' The policeman looked at her, saw her pallor, and took hold of her arm.

Was this her destiny, to meet tragedy head-on?

She didn't fight the policeman's firm grip. She walked on with a kind of terrible directness.

'That's him. That's him!' the policeman was saying, then like a miracle she saw Jay; a tall, lean and powerful form against a cobalt blue sky.

'It's okay, miss. *Really* . . . okay. Seems the pilot suffered a heart attack. Fairly young bloke too. As soon as the paramedics are finished with him we'll get him straight to hospital. I wouldn't like to think what might have happened if the Carradines didn't know a lot about different kinds of aircraft. Seems one of them brought it down.' It must have struck him as somewhat wry, because he gave a gruff laugh.

'*Jay!*' Brett's eyes held relief from a great anguish.

He was suddenly upon them, reaching for Brett and folding her into his arms. He pressed her head against his chest and spoke to the policeman.

'They're about ready to shift our pilot now. He's responding quite well, thank God.'

'Right, sir.' The constable executed a little salute. 'I expect my partner has finished off our report. Seems like a miracle the chopper wasn't a write-off.'

'It *was* rather like sky-diving,' Jay shook the hand that was thrust at him. 'Thank you for coming so promptly. Your efficiency probably saved Ray's life. I'll be speaking to the Commissioner in any case.'

'Thank you, sir.'

Brett lifted her head and the policeman smiled at her. 'Too bad you had to get such a terrible fright, miss. I understand you're getting married tomorrow. If I may say so, your fiancé had the greatest incentive possible to stay alive.'

They waited in a quiet little group, Brett and Jay, Elaine and Morton, while the semi-conscious pilot was put into the back of the ambulance. The T.V. cameraman was still filming, and Elaine drew a sharp breath.

'Wouldn't you think they'd leave the poor man alone? Is he going to be all right?' She lifted her eyes to her husband.

'God, as far as I was concerned he'd dropped dead. One moment Jay and I were talking, the next we were falling from the sky. I know one thing: if it had been just me up there, we wouldn't have stood a chance. I couldn't seem to think, I couldn't seem to move. It was all happening too fast. I tell you something,' he added. 'I'm going to get really fit. While I was staggering back in my seat, Jay was blasting into action. I know—I was there.'

Jay put a hand on Brett's hair. 'Why don't you

two go on? The car's here. Go home.'

'Thanks, pardner,' Morton sighed gustily. 'I don't mind if I do. Remember that time in North Queensland when we flew through an electrical storm? The goddamned plane was bucketing around like a brumby. It even rolled over in thick layers of clouds. All I could do was throw up and wait to die—didn't even care—while you had to stick there and pull it out of a dive. How come the two of us are so different? The only other man I ever knew so damned cool was J.B.'

'Do you want to go back with Mort and Elaine?' Jay bent to the quiet and pale Brett.

'I'm staying here.' She raised her arm and put it around him.

'Okay, so we'll go back to town with the T.V. boys. I promised them about two words when I caught my breath. I have to speak to Ray's wife and organise for the chopper to be brought in. It's nowhere near as badly damaged as I thought.'

It was almost two hours later before Jay was able to call it a day. Brett waited in his office and his secretary, unexpectedly motherly and solicitous, brought her tea and sandwiches.

'Eat them up, dear,' she advised. 'Something in the tummy counteracts shock.'

Eventually they were able to go.

Good wishes came from every side. Jay's manner could not have been more charming and carefree. He was a man with nine lives; a man on the eve of a blessed marriage. Brett nodded and smiled. It was quite, quite extraordinary. Her delicate features had assumed an ethereal quality with the intensity of her feelings. The shock of the morning was continuing to give her pain.

She wanted to feel elation, but she could not. She hadn't forgotten how fragile was the link to life; the way she had stared mesmerised at the upper section of the crashed helicopter. Remnants of that terror still held her in its steely claws.

'I'll change my clothes before we go back to the house,' Jay told her. 'We can have a few quiet moments together.' His voice was as calm as ever. 'Are you feeling all right, Brett?'

'Much better now.'

He continued to watch her with brilliant, hooded eyes.

While he changed out of his suit Brett wandered around the penthouse aimlessly picking up objects and setting them down. It had taken one startling and terrifying incident to make her realise she had been acting like a child who could not put her feelings into words. They had made passionate love, yet never once had she told him she was brimming with love for him. She had never found a way to say it. *Never*. Her childhood had marked her. She wanted so much to be free and unscarred. Love was the ultimate healer.

When Jay came back into the living room, so vivid and handsome, she went to him with a little cry.

'Tell me what's in your mind,' he begged her. 'This moment. *Say* it, Brett.'

'I love you.' The words were tight and choked.

'Say it again.'

'I love you.' This time they flowed more easily. 'Utterly, irrevocably. You are my life.'

He stared into her eyes for an endless moment, then cupping her face in his hands, he kissed her with a tenderness so exquisite she knew she would remember it for the rest of her days.

'That wasn't so terrible, was it?'

'No.' Her eyes were very soft and shining.

'Wait a minute, you're so small.' Jay swung her up and carried her back to a deep leather armchair where she curled up in his arms. Her gleaming hair fluttered against his neck and his chin.

'You could have been killed,' she said shakily.

'I wasn't!' This, very firm.

'All I could think was I'd never told you how much I loved you. I've withheld it from you all this time. It was crazy and self-destructive.'

'I'll have to admit it did give me a few bad moments.' He tilted back her head and kissed her on her forehead, her nose and her soft, tender mouth. 'In fact it might have driven me nuts. I dared not speak to you, touch you, until you were all grown up. God,' he groaned feelingly, 'all these years! I feel badly about your shock and upset this morning, but if it helped, and it obviously did, I'd be prepared to go through it again. Perhaps not to the same extent,' he smiled wryly. 'There's nothing like a nosedive to give a man wings.'

'*Don't!*' shivered Brett.

'At last I have you,' he said quietly. 'I can't remember a time when you weren't very special to me. A small girl with big, silvery eyes. All those years we could have enjoyed but for J.B. He was about as complicated a man as one could ever get. He told me once he'd make pretty damned sure *I* would never get you. All your life I think he mixed you up with your mother. But that's all over.'

'It *is*.' Brett lifted herself up and clasped her slender arms around his neck. 'Love can vanquish anything—hatred, enmity, pain. You've been my hero-figure, my champion, ever since I can remember. I never expected for you to love me, but miracles *are* possible in this world. Tomorrow we're going to be married. Tomorrow we fly back to Diamond Valley. From this moment I dedicate my life to you. I'm going to be the best wife in the world.'

'Perfect!' Jay gave her a blue, brilliant look. 'Remind me tomorrow night!'

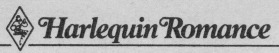
Harlequin Romance

Coming Next Month

2833 SOFTLY FLITS A SHADOW Elizabeth Duke
Jilted! A broken-hearted American embarks on her honeymoon cruise alone and attracts the attention of a fellow passenger, who assumes she's out to catch a husband. After what she's been through?

2834 TEMPEST IN THE TROPICS Roumelia Lane
The same meddling forestry man who's threatening her father's Guyanese timber plantation tries to stand in the way of a fiery daughter's plan to marry the one man she thinks could ensure her father's future.

2835 LOVE BY DEGREE Debbie Macomber
To make ends meet when she returns to university, a mature student plays housemother to three lovable Washington college boys. But instead of encouragement she gets the third degree from the owner of their cozy home.

2836 THE NIGHT IS DARK Joanna Mansell
Never get emotionally involved with clients—it's the number one rule for Haversham girls. But an assignment in East Africa with wildlife adventure writer Kyle Allander proved that love makes its own rules!

2837 THE APOLLO MAN Jean S. MacLeod
Still bitter over her childhood sweetheart's sudden departure from the Isle of Cyprus six years ago, a young islander is suspicious of his reasons for returning ... wary of her memories of love.

2838 THE HARLEQUIN HERO Dixie McKeone
A romance novel fan adopts her favorite heroin's sophisticated image to attract a living breathing hero. But her plan backfires when he takes a page from the same book to woo the woman of his dreams—another woman!

Available in May wherever paperback books are sold, or through Harlequin Reader Service.

In the U.S.
901 Fuhrmann Blvd.
P.O. Box 1397
Buffalo, N.Y. 14240-1397

In Canada
P.O. Box 603
Fort Erie, Ontario
L2A 5X3

ATTRACTIVE, SPACE SAVING BOOK RACK

Display your most prized novels on this handsome and sturdy book rack. The hand-rubbed walnut finish will blend into your library decor with quiet elegance, providing a practical organizer for your favorite hard-or soft-covered books.

Only $9.95

**Approximately
16" x 8"
when assembled**

To order, rush your name, address and zip code, along with a check or money order for $10.70* ($9.95 plus 75¢ postage and handling) payable to *Harlequin Reader Service*:

Harlequin Reader Service
Book Rack Offer
901 Fuhrmann Blvd.
P.O. Box 1325
Buffalo, NY 14269-1325

Offer not available in Canada.

BKR-1R

*New York residents add appropriate sales tax.

PATRICIA MATTHEWS

America's First Lady of Romance upholds her long standing reputation as a bestselling romance novelist with...

Caught in the steamy heat of America's New South, Rebecca Trenton finds herself torn between two brothers—she yearns for one but a dark secret binds her to the other.

Available in APRIL or reserve your copy for March shipping by sending your name, address, zip or postal code along with a check or money order for $4.70 (includes 75 cents for postage and handling) payable to Worldwide Library to:

In the U.S.
Worldwide Library
901 Fuhrmann Blvd.
Box 1325
14269-1325

In Canada
Worldwide Library
P.O. Box 609
Fort Erie, Ontario
L2A 9Z9

ENC-H-1

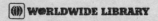 **WORLDWIDE LIBRARY**

Take
4 novels
and a
surprise gift
FREE

FREE BOOKS/GIFT COUPON

Mail to **Harlequin Reader Service®**

In the U.S.
901 Fuhrmann Blvd.
P.O. Box 1394
Buffalo, N.Y. 14240-1394

In Canada
P.O. Box 609
Fort Erie, Ontario
L2A 5X3

YES! Please send me 4 free Harlequin Presents® novels and my free surprise gift. Then send me 8 brand-new novels every month as they come off the presses. Bill me at the low price of ~~$1.75 each* with no extra charges for~~ shipping, handling or other hidden costs. There is no minimum number of books I must purchase. I can always return a shipment and cancel at any time. Even if I never buy another book from Harlequin, the 4 free novels and the surprise gift are mine to keep forever.   108 BPP BP7S

*$1.95 in Canada plus 89¢ postage and handling per shipment.

Name _____ (PLEASE PRINT)

Address _____ Apt. No. _____

City _____ State/Prov. _____ Zip/Postal Code _____

This offer is limited to one order per household and not valid to present subscribers. Price is subject to change.

ILP-SUB-1A

New This spring
Harlequin Category Romance Specials!
New Mix

4 Regencies—for more wit, tradition, etiquette ... and romance

2 Gothics—for more suspense, drama, adventure ... and romance

Regencies

A Hint of Scandal by Alberta Sinclair
She was forced to accept his offer of marriage, but could she live with her decision?

The Primrose Path by Jean Reece
She was determined to ruin his reputation and came close to destroying her own!

Dame Fortune's Fancy by Phyllis Taylor Pianka
She knew her dream of love could not survive the barrier of his family tradition....

The Winter Picnic by Dixie McKeone
All the signs indicated they were a mismatched couple, yet she could not ignore her heart's request....

Gothics

Mirage on the Amazon by Mary Kistler
Her sense of foreboding did not prepare her for what lay in waiting at journey's end....

Island of Mystery by Margaret M. Scariano
It was the perfect summer job, or so she thought—until it became a nightmare of danger and intrigue.

Don't miss any of them!

BPA-CAT87-1